CRUTCHES

CRUTCHES

PETER HÄRTLING

TRANSLATED FROM THE GERMAN
BY ELIZABETH D. CRAWFORD

Lothrop, Lee & Shepard Books   New York

MAP DESIGN BY GIULIO MAESTRO

Library of Congress Cataloging in Publication Data
Härtling, Peter, date   Crutches.
Translation of: Krücke. Summary: A young boy, searching vainly for his
mother in post-war Vienna, is befriended by a man on crutches and together
they find hope for the future. [1. Friendship—Fiction. 2. Austria—Fiction]
I. Title. PZ7.H26717Cr 1988 [Fic] 88-80400 ISBN 0-688-07991-1

CONTENTS

A FEW WORDS BEFOREHAND

This story takes place in the years 1945 and 1946, at the time the war instigated by Adolf Hitler had just come to an end. Many European cities lay in ruins. Countless numbers of people had lost their lives, and many others had been forced out of their homes. Under Adolf Hitler, there had been persecution and murder, offering proof of the bad saying: *The human being is the wolf of human beings; the human being is the merciless enemy of humankind.*

I have written this book to counter this adage. It is about the struggle to begin again when all seems to be lost. It is dedicated to Crutches and to Thomas, who have bequeathed to us the message that the human being is also the friend of humankind.

—P.H.

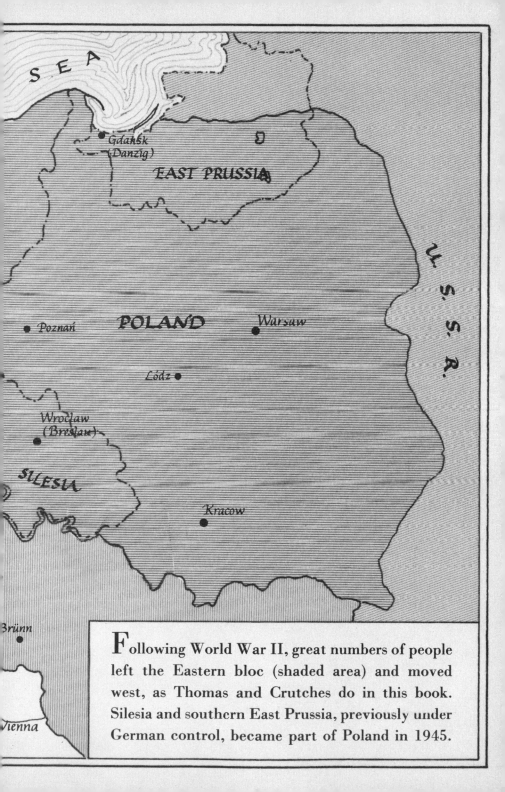

S E A

Gdańsk
(Danzig)

EAST PRUSSIA

U. S. S. R.

• Poznań

POLAND

Warsaw

Łódź •

Wrocław
(Breslau)

SILESIA

Kracow

Brünn

Vienna

Following World War II, great numbers of people left the Eastern bloc (shaded area) and moved west, as Thomas and Crutches do in this book. Silesia and southern East Prussia, previously under German control, became part of Poland in 1945.

CRUTCHES

♦

O N E

A Door Without a House

The woman sat on the stone doorstep, her kerchief pulled low over her forehead. She had piled her satchels and bundles around her like a wall.

What Thomas saw in front of him was simply crazy, hardly to be believed. It should have been the house he'd been looking for in Vienna for days on end. Before him now was nothing but the door frame in which the woman sat. She guarded an entrance that led to a mountain of rubble. She'd probably been sitting there for ages.

Maybe I'm dreaming, Thomas thought, and the woman isn't there at all. I'm just making her up.

Step by step he went closer. It had to be the house at Hellergasse 9 where Aunt Wanda had lived. Mother had drilled it into him. "Hellergasse Nine.

Don't forget it!" Only the house wasn't there anymore.

Thomas pressed his knapsack against his chest and
dared another step.

"Excuse me, is this Hellergasse Nine?"

When the woman lifted her head, he saw that she
wasn't so old at all, certainly no older than Mother.
But her face was strangely numb, and her eyes
seemed blind, as if she had looked into a fire for a long
time.

"Hellergasse Nine?" she asked.

"Yes. My aunt is supposed to live here, Mrs.
Wanda Watzlawiak."

"Here?"

"Yes," said Thomas, and added softly, "She did
live there."

"That could be," the woman murmured.

"Did you live here too?" he asked.

"If I only knew," she replied.

It was pointless. He wouldn't get any information
from her. Perhaps he would find someone in the
neighborhood who had some idea.

He mumbled "Good-bye" and was about to go,
when the woman began to speak in a changed voice,
bright and friendly. "Are you alone, boy?"

Completely surprised, Thomas didn't even have

time to make something up, as he had often done in the last weeks. "Yes," he said.

"Your parents? Your mother?"

"My mother disappeared suddenly. I lost her. We had to leave Brünn. We were trying to come here. To Vienna. To Aunt Wanda. We had been waiting for the train in Kolin for a long time. When it came, the people began shoving something terrible, and someone held onto me. They just about trampled me to the ground. Suddenly Mother was gone. I didn't know if I should take the train or not until someone dragged me into the car."

He saw again the grimacing faces of the people in front of him, felt the fear and anger rising in him, and came very close to howling.

The woman nodded, took one of the bundles on her lap, pointed to the cleared place on the doorstep, and invited him to sit beside her.

"But I won't be able to help you," she said.

He pressed himself in between the woman and the door frame, taking care not to touch her. She looked at him from the side, pulling the kerchief off her forehead.

"How long have you been alone?"

"I don't know."

He really didn't know. For a while he had counted

the days and sometimes asked people what day it was.

"Anyway, it was still wartime," he said. "And now it's peacetime."

The woman nodded. "A wonderful peace. No roof over our heads. Nothing to eat." After a while she said, "What are you going to do? Where do you want to go?"

He shrugged his shoulders. "I really wanted to find Aunt Wanda."

The woman began to laugh. It was a soundless laugh that shook her back and forth and made tears stream from her eyes. They were sitting so close together that he could not ignore the silent laughter but was shaken along with it. Had not fear held him fast, he would have liked to run away.

By degrees she grew calm again, then loudly drew in her breath and snorted. "No, no, my boy, I won't ever forget this 'really.' You have presented it to me. You've defined our whole lousy time with it: *Really* I must wait at home in my cozy house for my husband, Captain Kruse. *Really* this house here, in which your Aunt Wanda *really* lived, should still be standing. *Really* we are neither of us, you and I, here at all. *Really* I should soften my heart and say to you, youngster . . ."

She didn't finish speaking. She banged her elbow hard against his ribs, turned her head away, and said

in the old harsh voice that she had used at the beginning, "Go away! You can't dig out your Aunt Wanda.
You won't find anyone here anymore. Not your
mother, either. If you're hungry, go to that house
over there, the one that's still half standing. They
have soup in the basement."

Thomas didn't understand her. Why was she driving him away all of a sudden? He would have gone
anyway. Now she was treating him like someone who
wanted to rob her.

"All right. Good-bye."

He wriggled himself out of the corner between her
and the door frame, stood up, and looked up at the
kerchief. She had called her husband Captain Kruse.
"Good-bye, Frau Kruse," he said.

Then she lifted her head and smiled for the first
time. "*Really* Frau Kruse," she said, "but that was
formerly." She tapped her forefinger against his
chest. "Good-bye, boy. Eat yourself full over there.
See that you find your mother or a shelter somewhere."

It was hard for him not to turn around and look
at her. Now he was aware of how tired and heavy his
legs were. Just a few steps more, he urged himself.
Only a few more steps to that house over there. Perhaps they really had something to eat.

They did. And more. They even had a place to

sleep. The roomy cellar was filled with constant coming and going. Two women ladled thick soup out of a wash boiler that was obviously never empty.

Thomas held out his mess plate.

Again he was asked if he was alone. Again he told his story. Again the women's eyes filled with pity. "You'll find your mother." Of course he could remain overnight.

The old man who assigned the sleeping places opened a lath partition, showed him a small bed, and wished him good night. "You're lucky," he said. "Karasek's cellar has never been damp."

In a wooden box Thomas found a tattered army blanket. He had slept under many of those already. It smelled of cellar and somehow like shoe polish.

He paused only long enough to make himself comfortable, to cram his knapsack under his head, to spread the blanket over himself. His only thought was sleep, nothing more.

Thomas stayed in the cellar for two days, taking care not to attract attention. During the second night he was roughly awakened. He opened his eyes wide, blinded by the beam of a flashlight. Someone said, soothingly, "He's only a child. Let him sleep."

The hand that grasped him did not yield, however, but pulled him up. He was staring at a uniform jacket; a Russian soldier stood before him. "Papers," said the soldier.

"How can he have papers?" scolded the old man. "He's a child."

"A child," repeated the soldier, as if he were learning the word without understanding the meaning. "A child."

But the soldier continued to hold Thomas firmly by the arm. All at once the grasp loosened. The hand became friendly and stroked Thomas's shoulder.

"Good," said the soldier, but he still stood there, undecided. The old man, surprisingly brave, pushed him. The soldier yielded and disappeared.

In the early morning Thomas took leave of his hosts. The nighttime visit haunted him. He had heard a few days before that the police and the Russians were picking up unaccompanied children. That must not happen to him.

The women put bread and dried fruit into his knapsack. The old man accompanied him up to the street.

Thomas was not prepared for the brightness and the heat and laid his arm protectingly over his eyes.

"I hope you make out all right, my boy," murmured the old man, and gave him a shove. Thomas ran in the direction in which the old man had pushed him.

◆

Call Me Crutches

All of a sudden the one-legged man was there in front of him, as if he had grown out of the ground. Thomas followed him; he couldn't help it. The hopping, hurrying man hanging between two crutches drew him along like a magician.

The man was dressed like someone from a circus. Strictly speaking, he looked disreputable. On his head he wore a peaked cap that was too small. The blue jacket had certainly belonged to a good suit, only it was much too large for the one-legged man. It hung on him like a cloak that was too wide. The uniform trousers were a reminder that he'd been a soldier and never would be again. The left trouser leg was cut off at the knee and was fraying out. The man had hung a large cloth bag across himself, and it swung with every step of the crutches. It was stuffed full.

He must be one of those people who know how to
scavenge, thought Thomas. One of those who know
what there is and how to find it—horsemeat sausage
or fresh bread. He had very often met such fellows.
Mostly they were loners and placed great value on
staying by themselves.

Perhaps—the thought went through his head—
perhaps this one is different.

Suddenly the one-legged man disappeared, swinging between his crutches into a bombed-out ruin.
Thomas stopped, stunned. Perhaps the man had noticed him and wanted to lose him. Then in the distance he saw a cloud of dust, a jeep. Probably a
Russian patrol. And he knew this was why the man
had done the disappearing act. Thomas followed his
example, climbed over a crumbling wall, went into a
crouch, pressed himself against the warm stone, and
waited until the noise of the motor faded into the
distance.

When it was quiet, he stood up and peered over the
wall. The one-legged man was already under way
again.

Thomas kept a greater distance between them than
he had before. He didn't want to take the chance of
being discovered ahead of time and having the man
chase him off. He wanted to know where the man was
headed so purposefully.

The sun began to scorch, and he remembered how he'd frozen in the train when he was going through car after car, looking for Mother. That was a long time ago.

Now they were hurrying through streets that had remained undamaged by bombs. People were about. A streetcar bell rang, driving Thomas to one side. And then the city came to an end. The houses were lower, shabbier, detached from one another, no longer standing narrowly pressed together in a row. The sky broadened, and Thomas felt as if he could breathe more easily.

Before him spread an extraordinary landscape, a plain on which, as if on islands, stood single little houses or sheds, clumps of trees crowded together, and shaggy bushes that tried in vain to unite themselves into hedges. There was life on this plain. Wherever people moved, on foot, by bicycle, or with a wagon, little clouds of dust puffed up. They wandered, separated from one another, gathered together again.

The one-legged man sang. Thomas didn't understand a word, but it must have been a happy song.

They went quite a ways onto the plain. After a time the man swung himself over a small ditch, hopped up to a construction trailer without wheels that had

been mounted on blocks, opened a door, and disappeared inside.

Indecisively Thomas sat on a fieldstone in front of
the ditch. It was clear to him that it marked a bound-
ary he could not cross without permission.

He waited.

The man made himself busy around the trailer,
opened the window hatches. Suddenly he was standing in the doorway and looking over at Thomas.

Thomas stood up. He managed to hold the stare of
the one-legged man. The man had taken off the funny
jacket and also his shirt. A torn undershirt flapped
around an emaciated chest.

"Scram," said the man without moving his thin
lips.

Thomas didn't move and looked the man in the
eyes. They were brown eyes, lying in deep hollows.

"Scram," repeated the man. "Do a flit."

"What?" said Thomas. "What should I do?"

"A flit," repeated the man. "If you'll understand
better—disappear, bug off, beat it! Is that clear?"

It was clear, all right. But Thomas had no inclina-
tion to roam about on his own again, to be burdened
every evening with the fear of not being able to find
shelter, to have to beg for a piece of bread, a few
spoonfuls of soup. He'd had enough. He also had the

feeling that the one-legged man didn't mean what he'd said.

Thomas sat down on the stone again. He didn't take his eyes off the man opposite and stayed ready to leap and run.

The man leaned loosely against the door frame, grubbed in his pants pocket, fished out tobacco and a scrap of paper, began to roll himself a cigarette.

"Shall I help you find your legs?" he asked. He ran the tip of his tongue along the edge of the paper and pressed the cigarette together. He'd spoken to himself more than to Thomas.

Thomas relaxed. The way it looked, he'd almost won. Now he only had to wait and avoid saying anything wrong.

The man looked over and beyond him, as if he were watching some movement in the distance. The shadows sat like scars in his small, bony face.

"Are you alone?" he asked. He drew on his cigarette and blew the smoke out through his nose.

Next it will come out of his ears, thought Thomas. Then he answered. "Yes."

"Haven't you any parents?"

"My father was killed in action . . . at Woronesch," he added. That's what it had said in the newspaper: *Killed in action at Woronesch.*

This time the man blew the smoke through his teeth. "Woronesch, I know that place. A real sewer. Nothing but mud. And your mother?"

"She disappeared suddenly when we were waiting for the train together in Kolin. I couldn't find her anywhere. And not Wanda, either. Here in Vienna."

"Who is Wanda?"

"My aunt. We were going to meet there if we ever lost sight of each other. But the house isn't there anymore."

"Yes," said the man. "There are a great many that disappeared."

He seemed to be musing over all the people and houses that had disappeared.

I mustn't say anything dumb, Thomas thought, relieved. Then nothing will go wrong. Surely not.

He watched as the one-legged man, back pressed against the door frame, slowly sank to his haunches and sat.

"What's your name?"

"Thomas," he answered. "Thomas Schramm."

"How old are you?"

"In August I'll be thirteen."

"So. Soon, then," stated the man. He succeeded in flipping his butt so far that it fell hissing into the ditch of water.

"Are you hungry?" asked the man.

"Yes."

The man laughed and ran his hand down his only leg. "That really was a stupid question." He looked at Thomas again. His eyes became a fraction larger, sadder but also friendlier.

"There's no point in our setting traps for each other or fighting, is there? We're both poor as church mice, although I have never yet seen a poor church mouse. That's probably because I seldom go to church."

The man invited him to jump over the ditch, but Thomas was already over it. He could still take it all back, and Thomas wanted to forestall that. The man squinted his eyes, let him pass, and said, "Go right into this villa. My collecting bag is lying on the table. Get out the bread and the horsewurst. Get the knives and the plates out of the box by the stove and set the table for us."

Thomas didn't have to be told twice. He finished it all with unusual speed.

"Ready?" called the man.

"Yes," answered Thomas.

There was a surprising amount of room in the trailer. Everything necessary was there: a table, two chairs, a cupboard of nailed-together fruit crates filled with underwear and shirts.

In the corner there was a straw mattress on which the one-legged man slept.

"Help me move the table outside," said the one-legged man. "It's too stuffy here inside. And bring the chairs out."

They sat next to each other. The man cut the sausage, the bread, then laid the knife down and said, "It's better if we don't talk while we're eating. We'll enjoy every bite. But as soon as we're finished, I must say something to you."

And that he did, too, when the food was gone. "I have to tell you, you stink. You stink like a billy goat, like a barrel of manure water, like a beaver. You stink, my boy, of latrines, of sweat, of coal fires, of damp cellars. When, I ask you, was the last time you took off your things and washed them?"

"I don't know."

Thomas actually could not remember when he'd washed himself properly. Certainly he'd at least done his face and hands when there'd been an opportunity, in a little water basin in a house hallway or at a rain barrel.

"Listen," said the man. "Behind our villa there's a water pump. And on the stove there's a kettle, which you will fill, but only three-quarters full or the stove will collapse. Then make a fire with paper and wood, and as soon as the water is hot, wash yourself. Take off your rags and hang them out back on the line. Wash your underpants last. There's soap, too. Now go. In the meantime I'll clean up."

With anyone else Thomas would have protested. With the one-legged man he did not. He thought the man was all right. And Thomas had already noticed the business about the smell himself.

The one-legged man paid no attention to him as he got the water, set the kettle on top of the stove, and undressed. He was a little ashamed when he discovered the streaks of dirt on his belly and legs and his feet black to the ankles.

The hot water felt wonderfully good. The soap smelled good. The soft breeze that wafted through the window dried his skin.

He soaped himself again and rinsed himself off, rubbed his skin, couldn't get enough of it. Until the man warned him to save enough water for his underpants.

"You can take a shirt out of the box. Probably it will come down to your calves. I'll get used to the way you look."

Then the man didn't say another word until evening. He sat again in the doorway looking out onto the plain, where now there were scarcely any more little dust clouds moving. It was still warm. And though the sun was nearly on the horizon, the moon already hung suspended over them, a thin, pale sickle.

Thomas, lying in the grass beneath the clothesline, was finding it harder and harder to battle his weariness. Finally he jumped up, ran around the trailer, and asked the one-legged man without looking at him, "Where can I sleep?"

"Inside on the straw mattress."

"But that's your bed."

"As long as we don't get more to eat, we'll both fit on it. Lie down. Cover up with the coat that's hanging behind the door."

"Thanks," said Thomas, and because the moment seemed opportune, he dared to ask another question. "What's your name, anyway?"

"What's my name?" The man grinned with his whole face. "Call me Crutches; that's what I've been called for two years. Now go inside and leave me in peace." He began to roll a cigarette. "I haven't answered so many questions for an age. Good night."

"Good night," said Thomas. He could barely manage the few steps to the straw mattress. Until sleep overwhelmed him, one word echoed in his head. He said it to himself, and it made him feel peaceful and fearless. *Crutches.*

◆

T H R E E
Whereabouts Did
You Sleep?

The air was warm and thick in the trailer when
Thomas awoke. He thought it must already be late in
the morning. He stretched. He hoped he could lie
there for a while longer. Then came a loud banging
against the wall of the trailer. "Well, finally. Awake
now? Boy, boy, can you sleep!"

Thomas sat up and rubbed his thighs with his
hands. They hurt.

"You don't have to get up right now," Crutches
said reassuringly. "There's nothing the matter."

Thomas let himself fall back onto the mattress and
folded his arms under his head. He blinked his eyes
against the light. It had been ages since he'd awakened feeling so good. He recollected how in the middle of the night in Budweis a railroad worker had

discovered him in a tool shed and kicked him, and he'd been so frightened that he'd left his knapsack lying there. He'd had to lie in wait forever until he could run back across the tracks to the shed and find the knapsack.

"That was the first night," he said to himself.

"Tell," called Crutches. "But a little bit louder."

He made himself comfortable on the front steps.

"What shall I tell?" Thomas asked.

"Very briefly, how it all went on after that."

"All the places I spent the nights?"

"You express yourself fairly well. That's exactly what I meant. Where you slept. What holes you crawled into."

"After Budweis?"

"Yes, after Budweis."

"It was still the war."

"Did you get into any fighting?"

"Everything was all mixed up. Our soldiers were driving through the city with tanks and trucks, trying to get to the Americans. Others were marching to the front. And the strafers kept flying over. Then we would run into the houses or drop down in the street, under cars, behind tanks."

"You too?"

"Yes. I did what everyone else did."

"But you remained alone?"

"Yes."

Crutches thumped his crutches on the wooden steps. "Say a bit more once in a while. And say, 'Yes, Crutches!' We talk with each other like nameless ghosts."

"Yes, Crutches."

"And the next night?"

Thomas closed his eyes. It was like a movie. Except that he himself had a part in it. "I met some people. Outside the city. They were camping there, with five or six wagons and horses. There were a few boys, about the same age as me. They came from Silesia or even farther away. They said they didn't mind if I joined them. A woman gave me something to eat. I told how Mama suddenly disappeared from the platform in the station—"

He broke off. A word had frightened him. He'd avoided saying it until now. He'd never said "Mama" when he spoke of Mother.

"What's the matter?" called Crutches. "Swallow the cork?"

Crutches' joke helped. Thomas grinned. "Yes, something like that."

"So, keep on talking. A bit more concisely, my boy."

"They took me with them. I stayed with them for a few days. They knew I wanted to get to Vienna, to Aunt Wanda. Somewhere they decided it would be better if we separated. 'We want to go to Germany and you want to go to Vienna,' they said. 'First try to get to Schrems. Maybe trains will be running from there.' "

"And," asked Crutches a little impatiently, "were trains still running?"

Thomas shook his head. "No. But in the middle of the forest I met a man. He was really crazy. He was called Kasten. He was tall and thin. He had a lot of gold hidden in his shoes. Actually I wasn't supposed to know it. Only he kept looking behind him all the time, so I figured it out. I had to swear to him not to tell anyone. Not even if my life depended on it. I was frightened when he threatened me and waved his arms. Otherwise he was all right. He even had a great big whole ham in his knapsack."

Crutches interrupted him. "This isn't getting you anywhere. You'll never get to Vienna. So where else did you sleep?"

"I don't know," said Thomas. Crutches confused him with his impatience. It was as if he was supposed to cross out the days, as if there had only been nights. "This Kasten and I slept in the forest several times.

Then in Schrems, in the dark, we found an abandoned house. It even still had furniture in it. We
curled up in one bed—it was really comfortable. In
the morning, when we looked at the ceiling, we almost died of shock. Right over our heads the ceiling
was cracked apart and half of it was hanging down.
Kasten said, 'If we'd coughed, it would have fallen
down on us and buried us alive.' Then he grabbed me
and rolled his eyes. Really, he could do that. He
called me a bad omen. What's that, Crutches?"

Crutches considered briefly. "Nonsense, in any
case. But for your Kasten a bad omen is a kind of
warning."

"That has to be right. In fact, he said that we had
to part from one another. He always talked very
fancy. He gave me a bar of chocolate as a farewell
present. He was all right!"

"And then?"

"Then? Two or three times I slept in waiting
rooms. Never the whole night. There were always
patrols, and I thought it was better to disappear. I
also slept in the cab of a truck one time. And another
time, with a lady who spoke to me. That was in Horn,
I think. I was allowed to take a bath and then I slept
with her in a big double bed. That was great. Only in
the night the woman began to groan as if she was in

terrible pain. I got scared and got out of there. The Russians were already in Horn. When I first saw them, I just about crapped in my pants. And then one of them gave me something to eat. And a Russian truck gave me a ride for a little ways. Yes, and then I stayed overnight in a stable. In the morning the farmer found me and was mad. . . . Somewhere I'd heard the trains were running again. We waited and waited. It took a long time until one actually came. I had to sit up front in the tender. The coal kept sliding away under me and people had to hold on to me. The train finally got to Vienna. Here I mostly stayed in cellars. Once I even stayed in a smashed tank. But it was nasty because somebody had crapped in it."

"And how did you sleep here?" Crutches spoke so softly that Thomas scarcely understood him.

Thomas sprang up, ran to the door, and stood behind Crutches. He felt like leaning on him, but he didn't dare.

"Great," said Thomas. "Really great!"

Crutches pulled himself up on his crutches and inspected him, smiling. "It shows," he said.

Then all at once he became serious, as if he was annoyed with himself for being friendly.

"I have to leave now. Don't wait for me. I may stay

away overnight. You'll find enough to eat. Be careful. Don't make yourself conspicuous. There are bad types all over the place. So long, Tom."

He pulled a bag from beneath the trailer, hung it across his chest, nodded cheerfully to Thomas, and hopped along the field path with surprising agility.

Thomas swallowed a lump in his throat. He watched Crutches until he shrank to a dot on the distant highway and finally disappeared in tiny leaps into a cloud of dust.

It was not a new experience for Thomas to be left alone, to feel how the surroundings grew large and wide and he himself became small and miserable. But this time it was different. Crutches wasn't just someone he'd met by chance. Crutches was more. The friend he had wanted. Someone who knew what was what, who was able to deal with whatever unexpected might happen. If Crutches abandoned him, he knew for certain that nothing would matter anymore. And it did look as though Crutches was running out on him.

Throughout the whole afternoon Thomas crouched in the grass and stared at the road until his eyes burned. The day had become humid. Clouds began to well and pile up on the horizon.

He was afraid of thunderstorms. As a precaution he

moved the two chairs and the table underneath the trailer. Unease filled him and made him restless. He climbed into the little building and began to sweep the wooden floor with a frayed scrap of a broom. He smoothed the horse blanket on the mattress, lay down, jumped up, looked out to see heavy clouds lying over the plain, which was etched sharp in the acid yellow light.

"He's taken off," Thomas said aloud.

The thunderstorm approached quickly and broke over him. He pressed the door shut against the rising wind and barricaded it with boards. He covered over the little window with a sack. Only when the lightning flashed did his little cave brighten for a moment. He threw himself onto the mattress and pulled the blanket over himself. Father had always made fun of his fear of thunderstorms. "You act like a coward," he had said. *Coward* was a bad word. It sounded scornful.

Thomas was glad that no one could see him. He was shivering and couldn't stop. He was terribly afraid. Finally, when the thunder became softer, he fell into an exhausted sleep.

"Crutches?"

He awoke with the question, crept through the darkened trailer to the door, and pushed the boards to one side. It was clear that Crutches had not come back.

The trailer stood in a small pond. The sky arched blue over the fields and open meadows. They steamed under the sun.

Thomas stretched out his arms. The warmth enveloped him. It was a wonderful feeling. Still, without Crutches he couldn't enjoy it. He sat in the doorway feeling abandoned, considering whether he should run away, struggling with himself, and finally put off leaving till evening.

When evening came, he felt very calm. A picture-book moon gave a bright, chalky light.

In this light he saw a hopping line, still far away. It could only be Crutches. He forgot all caution and began to run. He ran, called, ran. When he reached Crutches, his face was wet. He gasped for breath and couldn't get any words out.

Crutches grasped him tightly in his arms, staggered, and mumbled over his head, "Not so hard, Tom. With only one leg, I won't survive your happiness."

On the way to the trailer Crutches asked how Thomas had passed the time. Had anything happened?

"Nothing," said Thomas. "Until the thunderstorm."

"And you survived that, too."

"Yes," replied Thomas. He felt a rush of pride, now that he was going along calmly and securely beside Crutches.

"Tomorrow," said Crutches, "tomorrow we must talk turkey with each other."

"Turkey—what do you mean?" asked Thomas.

Crutches stopped and hunched his shoulders so that his head sank between the crutches. "Turkey? That's a question. I mean, boy, we must talk about what is important for both of us. Clear?"

♦

FOUR
A Kind of Flight

"Now they're probably in for it!" cried Crutches the next morning.

There were shots outside. Thomas was instantly wide awake. In such moments he was aware that he was always on the point of being awake, even if everything seemed to be quiet.

Crutches leaned in the doorway and, keeping Thomas back with an outstretched arm, reported what was going on in the fields outside.

"Very clear that this had to happen sometime! Those people over there have hidden their potato sacks in the shed—like fat bait. And now a few hungry fellows are trying to get at them. Or maybe they're jobbers for black marketeers."

"Let me just look," Thomas begged.

Crutches pushed him back still farther into the trailer. "You'll soon have the opportunity," he said, "if they run in our direction. They may be thinking of hiding here."

Thomas crouched down and peered outside between leg and crutches. Some people were running over the fields and the unplowed acres. They kept changing their direction, doubling back—three still-tiny figures. Behind them were another three figures, moving somewhat more slowly, shooting with rifles and machine pistols—the pursuers. Sometimes the earth sprayed up near the fleeing people; then they sprang up or threw themselves down. From a distance it looked like a game. Thomas had the impression that the three shooters didn't want to hit their targets but were just making the three fellows run.

"Who did the potatoes belong to?"

"The Russians. They confiscated them."

"And the others want to steal them?"

"Yes. They're a little hungrier than the soldiers. It's always the same."

The figures grew larger. Now Thomas could make out their faces, faces with wide-open mouths, gasping for breath.

"They actually do have our hut in mind."

With unusual agility Crutches turned on his leg.

His crutch nearly hit Thomas, who was still gazing. Crutches snatched up his things. "Hurry, Tom," he urged. "There isn't much more time. Don't forget anything. There's your mess plate."

Thomas hastily packed his knapsack, pulled on his jacket, and jumped out of the trailer. He ran along beside Crutches, seeing only the path that wasn't one, grass, stones, dried-out out furrows; he stumbled and went on again. The warm air choked him.

"Do we have to run so?"

"For practice," panted Crutches. "Heaven knows how often you'll have to do this!"

Thomas stopped and looked about him. The three men had disappeared. The soldiers moved slowly up to the construction trailer, as if they were intentionally taking their time. Crutches also watched the scene. With his right hand he fumbled in his jacket pocket. He rolled himself a cigarette.

Thomas gripped Crutches' arm. "What's going to happen to them now?"

Crutches drew thoughtfully on his cigarette and spat out a crumb of tobacco. "Oh, nothing world-shaking. A hearing at the *Kommandantur,* perhaps a few days in jail. But the fear! That's bad."

"And what are we going to do?"

"Up there ahead—you can see it already—is the

last station on the tram line. We're going to ride into the city for the first time."

"And there?"

"There we'll try to hunt up your Aunt Wanda."

"But—"

"No buts, Tom. The whole company obeys me."

"I'm not a company."

"Lucky for us both."

Thomas began to laugh, and Crutches laughed with him.

♦

A Little Scrap of Heaven

Crutches' presence gave Thomas wonderful strength.
The great city no longer inspired fear in him.
Crutches knew his way around and led Thomas past
houses, churches, and streets as if they belonged to
him. He even dared to laugh in the great cathedral of
St. Stephan. And the overwhelming Hofburg looked
friendlier and more approachable when Crutches told
him that kings and queens no longer lived there, only
normal mortals like presidents and ministers. The
gloomy entrances to the gate towers, which resem-
bled gaping mouths and which Thomas had continu-
ally fled, under Crutches' leadership showed
themselves to be meeting places for traders or entrances to cellar establishments in which they served
everything that until then Thomas had only dreamed

about: thick soup, noodles, meat with sauce, even pancakes. . . .

Crutches explained how Vienna was arranged. It was divided into districts, he said. There was a first district, the inner city, and also a twenty-first, in which Aunt Wanda had lived.

"We live in a topsy-turvy world," said Crutches. "The Austrians have, of course, lost the war too, along with us Germans, but not to put too fine a point on it, they've actually won it. First of all, they're no longer Germans, as Adolf Hitler called them, but Austrians again. Second, they again have their own currency—the schilling. And third, the Americans, the Russians, and the English showed them a special honor, in that they all three entered Vienna together."

Thomas didn't understand everything Crutches— sometimes angrily, sometimes cheerfully—gave as explanation. The first time a jeep drove past him in which a Russian, an American, an English, and a French officer sat, he thought that this was probably the great honor that was being shown to the Viennese.

Crutches also said the honor brought luck. That is, the presence of the soldiers ensured that new wares were always being offered on the black market. "Just imagine, Tom, if we had no cigarettes, no coffee, no chocolate, no stockings for the ladies, no dried milk, and no dried eggs, and also no sweet potatoes, which are not to my taste, actually."

Crutches was a well-known personality in Vienna. "Here comes Crutches," people would say when they approached a group of men or turned in somewhere.

Crutches didn't let himself be drawn into conversation and took no interest in business. His mood had darkened. Perhaps his leg pained him; perhaps the flight from the construction trailer had annoyed him.

He was sitting with Thomas in a corner of a cellar café, away from his acquaintances. He searched for words, painted a gigantic figure eight on the wooden table with spilled beer, and then said, stopping every now and again, "How do I know, Tom, how long we'll stay together? In any case, we're not together permanently. We've got to find a solution. I've got to find a solution. Still, you are with me. From now on, you hear, you're my nephew, if anyone asks you. My nephew Tom. And I'm your uncle. I don't care what kind. Either a distant one or a close one, the brother of your mother or else of your father. You can decide that. . . . And if you cry now, say I'm mean, create a scene, I'll leave you here, and you can figure out how you're going to dig up your Aunt Wanda."

Every word hurt Thomas. Never until now had

anyone spoken to him this way. Never until now had
it been so clear to him that except for Crutches he
was alone, like a stray dog that anyone could beat,
kick, or capture. He bit his lip, pressed his shoulders
against the chair back, and stared past Crutches.

"Do you understand?" asked Crutches.

"Yes."

"I don't want to hurt you, Tom. But this is the way
it stands with us."

"Yes."

"Don't just keep saying 'Yes,' " said Crutches, imi-
tating him. His hand moved slowly across the table
and placed itself on Thomas's hand. It felt strangely
bony, but also warm.

"Shall I call you Uncle Crutches?"

Crutches almost jumped out of his seat. He shot
up, stood on his leg without wobbling, and let himself
fall again, shaking with laughter.

"Uncle Crutches! This can't be true. Boy, boy,
now all you're missing is Aunt Disaster. No, Tom,
stick with Crutches. Keep on calling me Crutches."

Thomas gathered courage. Perhaps now he might
succeed in learning more about Crutches. "What's
your real name?"

Crutches squinted the way he always did when he
was thinking about something that occupied him
completely. "You're right. I've nearly forgotten who

I was before Crutches. My name is—no, my name
was Eberhard Wimmer. Only don't you dare call me
Eberhard. I'm thirty-three years old and came from
Breslau. And where did you come from?"

"From Brünn."

"Both are lost to us, my boy."

"What did you do in Breslau?"

"I studied for a few semesters, national economy.
Then I became a soldier. And a few years later, a
cripple. In the meantime, so you can be a bit proud
of me, I was a first lieutenant. They hacked off my leg
in the beginning of 'forty-four. Gangrene. On the
retreat from Russia. I was in the hospital for quite a
while. Then I went back to Breslau, found a few
friends who didn't think much of the war and our
almighty Adolf. We drafted a flier, but we never got
to distribute it. Then I met Bronka. That's another
story. You'll get to know her."

Crutches pulled himself up on his crutches.
"That's enough. We'll go on over there to my friends,
the wheeler-dealers. Otherwise they'll get impatient.
At the same time we can see how convincing our
relationship is."

It worked. When the men asked about Thomas,
Crutches answered quietly and firmly, "This is my
nephew Tom."

Everyone seemed satisfied with this information.

Thomas sat there in that little joint all day long. The voices of the men began to seem far away. He no longer listened to them, just struggled against his weariness. If they chatter much longer, he thought, I'll fall asleep sitting up.

Crutches missed nothing. Softly, reassuringly he said, "Don't fall asleep; we'll break up very shortly. Then I promise you a little scrap of heaven."

The phrase stuck fast in Thomas's head. When the group finally did break up, Crutches warned, "It's after curfew. We'll have to be careful."

They hurried through narrow little streets. The night was bright. The sound of the crutches clumping was much too loud. Somewhere near St. Stephan's Cathedral Crutches halted before a house, rang, and pressed himself and Thomas into the entryway.

The door opened a crack.

A woman said, "Who can it be at this illegal hour?"

Crutches pulled Thomas in behind him. A light went on over the staircase. Thomas stood before an elegant young woman whose pale, very beautiful face seemed like a mask under black hair.

"This is the Tom I told you about," said Crutches. "And this is Bronka."

Bronka held out her hand, a hand light as a feather.

The other hand held her black dressing gown together over her bosom.

She smells of flowers, Thomas thought, and a little of cake, too. He breathed deeply.

"He's dog-tired," Crutches declared.

Thomas contradicted him. "Not anymore."

It seemed to Thomas as though he had fallen out of time. As though he hadn't been traveling on his own for weeks on end. He had forgotten that there were homes like this.

For a moment he curled up in one of the deep armchairs in the living room and closed his eyes. Music was coming from the radio. He thought, Just like home, when Mama sewed in the evening and I was allowed to read for a while.

He went into the kitchen and saw a loaf of bread lying on the table beside a dish of bean salad. His mouth watered. He restrained himself; he wouldn't begin to eat until Bronka invited him to.

Bronka and Crutches spoke softly and inquiringly with each other. Certainly they were speaking about him, what was going to be done with him. He strolled through the living room. They fell silent. He opened the door to the bedroom, felt their eyes on his back.

What he saw overwhelmed him completely: two beds, two proper beds, with big, white overstuffed

pillows and thick comforters. Overcome with longing
to sink into the wonderful white, to sleep endlessly,
he didn't notice that Bronka was standing next to
him, regarding this wonder with him. In an ethereal
voice she said, "You'll sleep here tonight, Tom. Together with Crutches."

Before that, though, they sat in the kitchen and
ate. Then they lounged in the armchairs in the living
room, hardly speaking at all, listening to music from
the radio, until Bronka, who kept disappearing behind a door, clapped her hands and summoned them
to a bath; the water heater was hot, the water was
hot, and the tub was already half full.

Thomas looked questioningly at Crutches, who
was beaming at Bronka. "Do you want to go first?"

Amazed, Crutches stared at him. "What's that supposed to mean? You think this regal hot-water boiler
is inexhaustible? One filling is just enough for the two
of us. And so is the bathtub. Maybe you're ashamed
in front of me."

"No, I certainly am not."

It wasn't shame that Tom felt. Rather fear. Fear
of the one-legged man, who suddenly seemed utterly
strange to him again.

"Let's try it!" Crutches pulled himself up on his
crutches and hopped into the bathroom.

Thomas just sat there, angry with himself for being indecisive. Finally Bronka helped him. She came out of the kitchen, looked at him, and shook her head. "Don't you want to bathe? Are you afraid of the water? As filthy as you are, my dear, there is no way you are going to sleep in my freshly changed bed without a bath."

He gave in and trundled off to the bathroom, accompanied by Bronka's cheerful laughter. Crutches was already stretched out in the tub. Thomas turned his back to him and undressed.

"Hurry up," Crutches urged. "The water's still good and hot."

Dropping his eyes, Thomas stepped into the tub. Crutches made room for him and tossed him a large sponge. "It's all here. Soap, shampoo! What the well-groomed gentleman needs. And now, look at me, Tom. Don't be foolish. Two men can share a tub."

Crutches was serious. He wasn't joking any longer.

"Good," said Crutches, "now look at me all over, a naked man with one leg. Look."

Thomas did as Crutches commanded, and yet he didn't. Frightened and with a feeling of disgust, he stared at the stump that hung from Crutches' body where once a second leg had been. Like a faceless creature, surrounded by numerous lumps and swellings, the stump moved now and again. Although

Thomas realized that Crutches was observing him, he was not able to tear his gaze away.

"Well, it's not exactly a beautiful sight," Crutches said.

Now the stump looked like a dead fish. Crutches' hand came swimming up and laid itself on it.

"When times get better, I'll have a prosthesis made. Then I'll only need a stick, and I'll throw my crutches in the corner and change my name. But until then—" Crutches stretched out and the stump came very close to Thomas. "A person can get used to anything. . . ."

Crutches squeezed a sponge over his head and his thin brown hair hung in strings over his eyes.

"No, not so. Sometimes the toes that I no longer have hurt. The minute I dangle them in warm water, they feel good."

He splashed Thomas, who had begun to scrub himself with his sponge.

"Probably you think I'm just making this up," Crutches went on. "How can toes that were thrown into a trash barrel by some orderly hundreds of kilometers away from here feel anything? But it's true. It's called phantom pain. I have a phantom leg. Understand? . . . Oh, let's leave it. Turn around and I'll scrub your back."

And Thomas did so obediently. Crutches was close

and trusted again. Thomas turned back quickly and rammed his head against Crutches' bony breast. Crutches snorted, submerged. The water sloshed out of the bathtub.

Their noise caused Bronka to appear. She had two long towels flying like flags. "Now, that's enough!" she said. "I'm not planning to spend the rest of the night mopping up your dirty water."

She obviously didn't think anything of seeing both of them naked. Thomas didn't resist when she wrapped him in the bath towel, pressed him to her, and rubbed him dry. She did it just like Mother. Then she handed him a man's shirt. She hadn't been able to find anything better; he should wear it for the night.

They marched in single file into the bedroom, Bronka first, he in the middle, Crutches at the end in a knee-length white nightshirt.

Thomas sank into the soft bed. His limbs, his body grew heavy. Meaningless dream pictures tumbled in his head, too many all at once. He scarcely managed to say good night, but he felt how Crutches' hand closed on his arm. Bronka left behind a small fragrant cloud. It smelled of cooking and a wonderful perfume.

Uncle Crutches

They were talking and talking. Voices kept buzzing
around him. As hard as he tried, he couldn't understand what they were saying. But he knew they were
talking about him.

He didn't consider leaving the marvelous bed.
Crutches was no longer lying next to him. Thomas
pulled the covers up to his eyes and began to sweat,
for the warmth of the day was streaming through the
open window. Cries rang out from the street below,
and occasionally the rumble of a car.

"Crutches!" he called softly.

No one answered. He didn't really want an answer,
just to make himself comfortable in bed for a while
longer until everything was the way it used to be.
Until Mother walked into the room to shake him out

of the feathers. Or else Crutches did. Somehow the two of them belonged together for him. But it wasn't Mother and Crutches, it was Bronka and Crutches who were talking in the next room. Thomas sat up. Now he could understand them.

Crutches seemed to be very excited.

"But I've already found out from the police in District Twenty-one that this Wanda was killed; she's not alive anymore. How many times do I have to tell you that, Bronka? Who's going to look after him?"

Bronka tried to calm him. "You're making assumptions, Crutches. They've told you that this Wanda is missing. She could also be alive. Why not?"

"Oh, you." Crutches gave in.

Thomas could see him, how he deflated, ran both hands through his hair. He was ready to jump out of bed and run to Crutches. But then Bronka spoke, terribly matter-of-factly, as if it had nothing to do with him at all. "You've become so attached to this boy. . . ." That's right, thought Thomas, Crutches likes me, even if he's hard on me sometimes. "You can't just drag him along with you like that. His mother is looking for him."

This was a surprise to Thomas. Until now it had never occurred to him that Mama might be looking for him. He had just been looking for her. And for Wanda.

"She'll certainly have contacted the Red Cross," Bronka said.

"Yes," Crutches agreed, "probably."

"You have to register Thomas there. In any case."

"Yes," said Crutches. "Certainly."

"Besides, you know they're gathering up parentless children. They're setting up homes for them in Grinzing, in Wiener Neustadt."

"Yes," said Crutches.

"So there's no point in putting things off. Every day it will be harder for you to part with the boy. Or do you perhaps have it in mind to take him back to Germany with you? You want to have a burden like that around your neck?"

"Bronka—" said Crutches. But he got no further.

"No!" shrieked Thomas. They shouldn't be talking about him that way. As if they were talking about a piece of baggage that they were going to leave somewhere. As if Crutches hadn't taken him in. "No," he cried once again in his fear, in his rage.

Crutches was already standing in the doorway. Bronka was a few steps behind him. She pressed a fist against her mouth, as if she wanted to cram back everything she'd said.

She looked at him with her large gray eyes.

Crutches shook his head angrily. "How thoughtless of us. Forgive us, Thomas. But—" He stopped, let himself sink between the crutches as he always did when something distressed him, and then continued in a softer, hoarse voice. "You're right. We can't help it that it's turned out this way. I ought to have sent you away at once. At the beginning I didn't care about you; in fact you were even burdensome. Just another stray youngster. But now?"

For Thomas the questioning "now" embraced everything they had experienced together in the last few days.

"Now," said Crutches, "we're just beginning to realize that we've acted like children. Without considering anything. Surely your mother will be looking for you. Certainly, if she's had the chance, she'll have informed your relatives. You still have grandparents, aunts . . . ?"

Thomas nodded. Funny, he'd never even thought of them.

Excitedly Crutches shoved Thomas ahead of him. They sat down together on the couch.

"We mustn't put it off; we should get it behind us quickly—that will hurt the least."

Thomas noticed that Crutches wasn't letting him say a word; he was trying to fend off gloom with his activity.

"We'll write it all down!"

He asked Bronka for paper and pencil and interro-

gated Thomas. About his grandparents; about Uncle
Eugene, Mother's brother, who was missing in Africa;
about Father's sisters, whose addresses Thomas
didn't know. When Father had been killed. What
Mother's maiden name was. Thomas answered as well
as he could.

When Crutches had gone through all the questions,
he urged him to hurry. "Get dressed, Tom. Hurry,
hurry. No reason to be tired after twelve hours of
sleep!" He hurried Thomas into the bathroom, didn't
let him out of his sight, helped him get dressed,
rushed him ahead of him—amid laughter from
Bronka—grabbed a piece of bread from the kitchen
and pressed it into his hand, and then they were
running down the stairs.

As if he were wound on a spring, Crutches hastened
ahead of Bronka and Thomas in great leaps. The
houses appeared to hop in the opposite direction.
Thomas wasn't able to get his bearings. Only when
they crossed Stephansplatz and turned into the Gra-
ben did he recognize anything again.

"Crutches," he said, so softly that Crutches didn't
hear him. He didn't mean the Crutches who was
hurrying on ahead but the other cheerful, friendly
one with whom he had sat in the bathtub the night
before.

Unexpectedly Crutches halted in a narrow street.

Sunk in thought, Thomas ran into him. Crutches barely managed to keep his balance.

"Now the young devil is even knocking down cripples!"

It was supposed to be a joke, but Crutches' face remained grimly serious.

"Here we are. This is where the International Red Cross is." He took a deep breath, looked at Bronka for help, and said, "Let's get it over with!"

That was a good idea, but once inside the front door they got no farther. All the way up to the second floor people were sitting on the steep stairs, shoulder to shoulder. The people gazed at them indifferently, and one of the waiting crowd said, "You'll have to be patient, just like us."

Crutches ran his hands through his hair and let his glance travel up and down the stairs. "I've already had a load of patience in the last few years," he said.

He leaned against the cracked wall of the hallway, pulled Thomas over next to him, fumbled in his right jacket pocket, and pulled out a cigarette.

Apparently Bronka had had only bad experiences with patience. She stood first on one foot, then the other, and rubbed her cheeks with her hands until they glowed. "I'm not going to be able to stand this," she murmured, and she put her hand on the doorknob. "Don't be angry with me. I'm leaving. You'll be all right alone, won't you?"

The door closed behind her.

It was hot on the stairs, and it reeked of tobacco, sweat, and dirt. Now and again people would squeeze together to let someone who'd finished in the offices above pass through on the way down.

"Look at that," said Crutches. "Half of humanity is looking for someone or being looked for. Mothers are looking for children, wives are looking for husbands, children are looking for parents. And all this because 'the greatest general of all time' wanted to conquer half the world."

Thomas didn't like it when grown-ups talked about the Führer that way. Before grown-ups had always admired him. But Crutches certainly didn't. Probably because of the leg. Perhaps he'd had something against Hitler anyway. Thomas remembered how Father had come home from the Front on furlough. They had listened to the radio. There were reports of victory on certain portions of the Front. Father turned the radio louder and said at the end, "You only have to believe in the Führer. Then it will be all right!"

He'd been killed soon after that. Mother had shut herself in the kitchen. Thomas had sat in front of the door and had had to wait a long time until she came out, changed somehow, quieter, indifferent.

Gradually Crutches and Thomas worked themselves up the stairs, moving from step to step. Then upstairs in the hallway they inched along on benches.

When they finally stood in front of the older man who had evidently entrenched himself behind a mountain of papers, it went very quickly.

"Do you want to leave a message?" asked the man.

"Yes," said Crutches. "The boy here is looking for his mother."

"Are you his father?"

"No, his father was killed in action."

The man looked at Thomas and indifferently through him. "Where are you staying?"

Thomas pointed to Crutches. "With him."

"You have shelter and are registered?"

Crutches nodded and added a dry "Yes."

The man from the Red Cross seemed to be content with that.

"Are you related to the boy?"

"Yes."

"Are you registered?"

"What?" asked Thomas.

"Yes," Crutches answered for him.

The man took two papers out of a drawer. They

were forms for the international search bulletin. "Fill these out carefully and completely and send them to the address listed in Geneva. If anything comes of it, either good or bad, you will receive notice. That will be all, I expect," the man said.

Crutches was already on the way to the door, Thomas with him. Outside in the corridor he raised a crutch high, leaned gently against Thomas, and gave him a poke with his elbow.

"And now?" asked Thomas.

"Now we'll report to Bronka."

"And the homes Bronka spoke about?"

"There'll be no question of that for you."

All at once the wind seemed somewhat friendlier and cooled his face. The sky was bluer, the houses looked newly washed, and the people coming toward them appeared to rejoice with him over his newly acquired uncle who wanted to be called just plain Crutches.

◆

Three Persians
for Five Piglets

Life with Crutches and Bronka was never dull. There was always coming and going in the apartment. Often the doorbell rang and a new, odd, crazy visitor would appear. In time, Thomas learned to know them better.

Ferdi, for instance, who never just walked through the door but always made an entrance.

Applause was guaranteed every time.

Everything about Ferdi was polished: the hair smoothly combed back, the guileless round face, the same always-spotless suit, and the black patent shoes. He was, he insisted, a cavalier by profession, and that suited him. In fact, he lived off the black market. He had the reputation of being able to get anything anyone wanted. Bronka didn't like him, but Crutches wouldn't hear anything against him. He had the best connections; you could steal horses with him. Bronka considered that an exaggeration. Ferdi would tell you they were horses, but if you looked carefully, they would turn out to be goats, at best.

Boris, another visitor, at first inspired fear in Thomas. He was a Russian officer and very conscious of his rank. He scarcely said hello. He talked only in Russian with Bronka. If he addressed Crutches—and that happened seldom anyhow—she had to translate. Thomas remained invisible to Boris until he had a fever one time and was sick in bed. Then an entirely transformed Boris visited him and talked to him and, finger on his lips, pushed a bar of chocolate under the covers.

Still, Crutches maintained that no one would get anything past this mammoth in uniform. . . .

On the other hand, everyone liked David. Bronka had known him for a long time. Sometimes, when he was especially sad, she called him "my little owl." He looked like one, too. A thin little manikin, with a bald-shaven head stuck on his neck. Whoever looked into his large, watery gray eyes became lost in their depths. David, too, had to do with opaque dealings. Like Ferdi and Boris, he was operating outside the law. He mainly concerned himself with people who didn't have passports and countries, Polish and Hungarian laborers who were living in camps outside the city.

Bronka and David were Jews. When Thomas learned that from Crutches, he didn't want to believe it. He remembered that his teacher had depicted Jews as dangerous monsters and had written the words *antisocial parasites* on the blackboard in large letters.

When Erika turned up, Crutches was always very attentive. She knew far more than was in the newspapers. Her favorite sentence was, "I'm bursting with news." That seemed like a real danger, for her breast would swell with pride and excitement. Crutches would express interest and suggest that first she should sit down and have a little drink with him.

She would clink glasses with Crutches and then command, "Now listen to this!"—whereupon a torrent of news would rattle out of her. To Thomas it remained a terrible confusion of names and events. But Crutches had no trouble understanding. Now and again he would interrupt Erika.

With just such a conversation their "swinish adventure" began.

"What did you just babble about a pig?" asked Crutches.

Erika was disconcerted and lost her train of thought. She twisted her hands, her breast heaved.

"Where was I? What pig? How did you get to pigs, anyhow, Crutches?"

Crutches stuck with it relentlessly. "You just mentioned it. Pigs somewhere in the Wienerwald. Pigs that we could buy or barter for. Are there really pigs? How many are there?"

No one was as good as Crutches at unraveling Erika's narrative tangles. Without further help she found the pigs. "Yes, yes, the pigs. There are five. Alive, almost bacon. Although I haven't seen them myself, it's reliable. The owner wants at least three presentable Persians or two first-class ones."

"She means oriental rugs," Crutches explained to Thomas.

"He's already rejected some offers. He apparently has taste, or he's acquired the taste." She giggled, pleased at the wordplay.

"So we're not the first?" With his forefinger Crutches painted invisible question marks and exclamation points on the tabletop. "Does it make any sense to deal with him, then?"

"Oh, yes!"

Thomas thought she became even better looking in her excitement. She glowed. A wild gleam came into her eyes. "You're of an entirely different caliber, Crutches. I have the address."

Then it went back and forth. "Who'll take care of

getting the Persians? Ferdi? Boris?" Bronka had objections to both and came up with someone better. "How do we get there? How about the checkpoint? The place is in the Russian zone. Who'll drive?"

"That's all taken care of." Erika clapped her hands, stood up. "You worry about the Persians! I'll worry about the transport. Tomorrow at three, punctually at three, a driver will be waiting in front of the house."

She disappeared. Crutches followed her a little later. He was going to round up the Persians.

Thomas didn't dare ask how and from whom. Crutches wouldn't have told him anyway. "It's enough," he always said, "if I converse with my bad conscience alone. I don't need a round of discussion as well."

The Persians were lying in the hallway the next day, three long sausages of carpet. Erika, too, had kept her word. Punctually at three the driver rang the doorbell.

Although Crutches had enjoined him to keep out of this risky affair, to pass a lovely day with Bronka, Thomas ran downstairs with him. He helped to load the rugs.

Erika had dug up a marvelous team. The driver seemed just as rusty as the car. Attached to the car, which was missing the glass in the side windows, was a wooden box trailer on two hard-rubber tires. They had to bend the rolls of carpet to fit them inside.

There would be enough room for the pigs.

"What about the boy?" asked the driver as Crutches squeezed himself groaningly into the car.

"What about him?"

"He could help us. A child is always good at a military checkpoint."

Thomas didn't wait to be asked twice. In no time he was in the backseat. He felt wonderful, prepared for any adventure. It didn't bother him in the least that it had begun to rain. He was sitting half in dryness and in the company of two men who knew their way around.

Crutches remained stubbornly silent. The driver kept trying to get a conversation going. "My name is Emil Redlich," he said. Crutches made no move to introduce himself.

Thomas became more and more occupied with protecting his bottom from bruises. Bombs and grenades had left their marks on the highway everywhere. The rubble had been cleared off to the side, but still the car bumped into holes and over trenches. The trailer creaked as if it were about to fall apart the next minute. When Thomas saw that Redlich was headed for one of those little craters, he held himself up by his arms and avoided the bump. Gradually he got better at it.

Destroyed houses appeared along the road less and less often. Farmers were working in the fields. Now and again a military vehicle came toward them.

They saw the first patrol from quite a ways off. Red Army soldiers were standing in the middle of the road and waving. Redlich remained the picture of calm. He pulled on the brake, but the car didn't come to a complete halt and was shoved a little farther along by the trailer . . . right up to the boot-tips of the soldiers.

"That wasn't what the inventor had in mind." Angrily Redlich pulled on the brake.

Crutches broke his silence. "That's right," he growled, and he sat up higher in his seat. They fished in their pockets for their papers.

"Paper," one of the rain-soaked soldiers demanded. "Paper!" He took the passes back to a shed at the edge of the road.

Thomas watched him page through the identity papers. How often during his wandering he had seen people being asked by soldiers for their papers. Maybe soldiers who had conquered were overcome with an insatiable desire to read passes. Maybe they conquered all over again when they demanded a pass from someone.

The soldier came back, pressed the passes into Redlich's hand, and gestured with a movement of his head that they might go on. The car sprang forward with a leap.

"They'll pay you back on the return journey. You splashed all over the poor fellow."

Crutches had decided to be talkative. Perhaps only to ask Redlich why the soldiers hadn't looked in the trailer.

Redlich's neck swelled. "I have an official pass. They had to realize that they would be interfering with an official transport."

"Then it's all clear to me," said Crutches with understanding. "This means Boris, our guardian angel, has a hand in the affair. And he hasn't even gotten his nose dirty over it. Who would accuse him of wrongdoing when he's helping to alleviate the hunger of his comrades?"

The ride seemed endless. They wound through little settlements on small forest roads, up hill and down dale, were checked several times by military patrols and allowed through.

"We'll be coming back in the dark." Crutches spat his vexation out the window.

Even this didn't shake Redlich out of his calm. He had calculated that. It was all the same to him.

They arrived. But not, as Thomas had expected, at a farm. There were no stalls and no barn, but a collection of unprepossessing wooden huts swimming in mud puddles, surrounded by a dark forest of pines.

Before one hut stood two men. They must have been twins. They both wore boots and riding breeches and checked shirts; both had black, curly hair like fur falling over their foreheads; each had a beard around his mouth that looked as if it had been glued there. They appeared to have planned to be mistaken for each other.

Thomas expected to see them move at the same time. That didn't happen. One came forward. The other remained standing in the background, arms folded across his chest.

"The boy stays in the car," said Redlich. Crutches agreed.

It all went very quickly, almost wordlessly. The men greeted each other with a handshake and then went to the trailer. The twin who'd first stayed back now joined in. Together they dragged the rugs into the nearest little house.

The door closed behind them.

Then it opened again.

One of the twins came out and let out a peculiar high whistle. Then he disappeared. After a while he appeared again. Of course it could also have been the other one. Everything was repeated, only the whistle sounded different. And this time it had an effect. It was the signal for a puzzling, disconcerting scene. Two barefoot women, paying no attention to the puddles, sped up to the car. They pulled a little wagon behind them in which two squeaking crates were sliding back and forth. They stopped beside the trailer and stowed away the load. There were no wasted movements. Then they were off again and disappeared behind the huts.

The twin whistled a second time. The door opened. The other twin and Redlich and Crutches walked out. At the end the twins were again standing next to each other. Thomas squinted up his eyes so that he saw them blurrily. They moved together and nearly became one.

Crutches pulled him out of the car. "Come on, we both have to ride behind in the trailer. The crates ought not to move around too much, so we have to hold them somehow. Otherwise the pigs will go crazy."

They crept into the trailer. Redlich closed the tailgate behind them. There was enough light coming through the cracks between the boards to see by.

Thomas examined the load. "These aren't pigs, Crutches! These are piglets. They stuck you."

Crutches shoved one of the crates against the side with his back. "Oh, well. If it comes to sticking people, we stuck them, too. We didn't give those brothers any real oriental carpets, only good imitations at best."

Thomas didn't like it when Crutches spoke that way.

Crutches rubbed his leg stump thoughtfully. "Yes, we have come down," he said almost to himself. "In these times what does it mean to say, 'Stay on the rug—play by the rules'? Rugs can't be eaten. Piglets can."

At that moment Redlich started the car. The trailer bounced from one unevenness to the next. Thomas was able to keep the crate from sliding only with great effort. This had no calming effect on the piglets. They squealed as if they were about to be killed.

"Oh Lord, this is going to be some journey," groaned Crutches.

It was. They slid, flew around the trailer, held tight to the crates, were pressed and pushed by them. In the beginning the piglets squealed without interruption, but after a few kilometers they squeezed close to one another, exhausted, and only squeaked softly now and again.

"This damned box, this mad Redlich! Soon it's going to be the same for us as for these animals," raged Crutches. His crutches had become independent and were flying around his ears. "Catch at least one of these things and sit on it, Tom."

They stopped twice at very short intervals. They could hear voices outside. Crutches laid a warning finger on his lips. The quiet induced some of the piglets to begin to squeak again. Thomas expected the tailgate to be opened and the two of them to be dragged out by soldiers, and the piglets, too. But Redlich was wily. As soon as one of the piglets got loud, he raced the engine and raised his voice. The soldiers probably thought he was an idiot. At any rate, the ploy worked. They got through without the trailer being checked.

The small victory made Redlich overconfident. He was now driving on tracks that were merely distant relatives of highways. The trailer was in the air more than it was on the ground. It bounced, snapped to the left, snapped to the right as the load was divided and then slid, then came down with such force that the boards no longer simply creaked but began to split.

There was no more noise from the piglets.

But there was plenty of noise from Crutches. Beside himself with rage, he bellowed over the racket, demanded that Redlich stop at once, otherwise he'd make him move, show him what a raking-over was— no, what a crutching was. "You nitwit! You pin- head!" he cried, then ran out of breath. He subsided and asked Thomas if he could stand this torture a little longer.

"It's all right, Crutches."

Thomas wasn't lying. The whole trip seemed un- real to him. As if he were dreaming it—Redlich and the trailer, the twins, and the two barefoot women. Perhaps, the thought shot through his head, he was only dreaming an unending long dream, was sitting in the train with Mother, and soon she would wake him. And he would need a while to forget the dream.

Still, there was the cursing Crutches. Still, there was the stink of pigs. And there was no more light coming through the cracks. It must be dark outside. They sat in the dark in the trailer, prisoners of Red- lich's madness.

Suddenly the trailer was no longer bouncing and jerking in one plane. It shuddered, shook, sank a bit forward, sank a bit backward, became a carousel, turned on its own axle, bumped forward, slid. One of the crates pressed Thomas against the wall. He held fast to it, but he was dragged straight across the floor by it and remained hanging on to Crutches, who quickly snatched Thomas to him.

First Thomas didn't understand what Crutches was stammering. Then it became clear to him: The trailer had come loose from the car and was rolling along on its own.

There was a crack. The trailer tipped forward. Crutches slipped straight ahead, grabbed him, but could not keep one of the crates from ramming Thomas in the back.

In the strange silence Thomas heard himself groan.

Crutches pulled himself up and tried to open the door, which now lay over them like a ceiling. Once again his crutches showed themselves to be all-purpose work tools. Propping himself on one, he pushed up the trapdoor with the other.

They looked out over the treetops into a wonderfully clear starry sky. They breathed deeply. Thomas climbed out of the trailer and then helped Crutches out. They were stuck in a forest. The trailer was caught in a gap between two trees.

Timorously the piglets began to squeak.

Thomas leaned against a tree. His whole body trembled as if he were cold.

Crutches stroked Thomas's head. "That will pass soon," he said. "The fear has to shake out first."

Then, probably to allay his own anxiety, he delivered a little speech. "Relax. It's all gone well so far. Oh, Redlich, how little you deserve our trust! What have you done to us? Where have you dropped us, you two-bit torturer's apprentice? How do you think we are going to find our way out of this forest with the piglets?"

As if he'd been called, Redlich appeared between the trees, waving his arms, protesting his innocence. "Listen to me, Crutches. Don't blame me. The trailer hitch didn't hold. I took this way to avoid the checkpoint, don't you understand?"

Crutches spat and did not respond to Redlich, who listened with obvious relief to the squeaking of the piglets. "Well, at least nothing happened to them."

"Your good will, Redlich, is immeasurable," observed Crutches. "Might you also be able to find the time to concern yourself about *our* condition?"

Redlich spared himself the trouble. He got busy with the trailer, tried to right it, and finally managed to do so, groaning and cursing. Crutches didn't help him. "What have you in mind, Redlich? Are you planning to walk? Are we going to carry the crates of pigs back to Vienna?"

Redlich waved. "The car is over there."

They carried the crates over to the car. They placed them inside without any difficulty.

"Why, I ask you, did we need the trailer?"

Redlich rubbed the back of his nose with his hand. "How was I supposed to know that your Persians would only be enough for piglets? I was figuring on regular pigs."

Dawn broke. Once they got into Vienna they felt the sun. Thomas had slept for the rest of the journey. Redlich dropped them in front of the house and promised to deliver the meat and the sausage in the next few days.

They didn't have to ring. Bronka was waiting for them in the open doorway. She had tears in her eyes. She looked even tinier and more fragile than usual. She rushed to Thomas and hugged him. "You two are late! I've been afraid something had happened to you!"

Thomas pressed his face into her shoulder. It was grand that Bronka was so concerned about him. Now he knew that she liked him. And he liked her very much. Almost as much as Crutches.

Crutches had already taken his place at the kitchen table and was chewing. "I have an appetite, I'm telling you! We couldn't nibble on the pigs."

Bronka showed a strained smile. "What you do to a person! I fixed supper for you, then a snack for the night, and now breakfast. Was that necessary?"

"Ask Redlich," answered Crutches.

They ate. The coffee smell filled Thomas's nose. He felt happy in a way he seldom did. Maybe it was this adventure, he thought.

Bronka was of a different opinion. "This is an end of this madness," she said. "You will find a job, Crutches, or go back to Germany with the next transport. And I will devote myself to my children."

Thomas was alarmed. What children did she mean?

"Do you have children?" he asked.

"No." She drank a swallow of coffee and then said, "I don't have any. Don't worry. I'll stay here as long as you need me. And sometime Crutches can tell you about my children who aren't mine."

♦

Only Five More Weeks

Crutches called at the Red Cross twice but without success. So far no one had responded to the search bulletin.

"Now you've already been with us for longer than a month," observed Bronka.

Sometimes Bronka and Crutches spoke about Thomas as if he weren't sitting right there at the table.

"Tom must go to school," Bronka said. "And we ought to register him with the police. Otherwise he doesn't exist. He'll be unknown officially."

"What harm can that do?" answered Crutches. "He's avoided the officials and the authorities up to now."

"It could be interpreted wrong. They could accuse

69

us of wanting to hide Thomas to claim him for ourselves. You take everything so lightly, Crutches, and
never think of the consequences."

"Why should I go to school," Thomas asked, "if
Crutches is going to take me back to Germany anyhow?"

"Because otherwise you'll be dumb, Tom. Didn't
you say that your father was a teacher? I can't just
leave you to Crutches. He'll only teach you nonsense."

That wasn't so. She had no idea. She didn't know
how unhappy Crutches was about not being able to
find anything reasonable to do. And how lovingly he
spoke of her. Perhaps she was exaggerating to jolt
Crutches out of his calm and didn't notice that it was
a dangerous, depressed calm. Crutches had long ago
had enough of the black market business. He envied
her her work helping those parentless little brats, as
Crutches called them, those poor little kids. He, too,
was one of Bronka's children, Thomas thought. But
she would no doubt dispute that.

Why Bronka left them alone on many days, why
she sat over piles of papers in the evening and typed
long letters and reports on a beat-up old portable
typewriter, Thomas learned—like many another
story from Crutches' life—on one of those endless
lazy mornings of lounging in bed.

When Bronka left the apartment early, a deep, contented humming might come from Crutches' bed. This was the invitation to a morning of lounging in bed. What came next almost never varied.

"How would it be to have a nice big breakfast right now?"

Thomas didn't have to answer. Crutches took his agreement for granted. He would shove himself out of bed, go into the kitchen, busy himself there, whistling and humming, and finally summon Thomas to come, if you please, and get the damn tray, which he could not balance.

Crutches insisted on his rule: No talking while eating!

When there were only the remains of coffee in the bottoms of the cups, Thomas's role was to begin with a question. Then Crutches would go on from there. And he didn't like to be interrupted.

"Why were you living out there in the trailer and not here with Bronka? Did you have a fight?"

Crutches rolled himself a cigarette, lifted it up and looked at it after he'd lit it, and declared to Thomas and himself, "You shouldn't smoke in bed!" Then he shoved the pillow behind his neck and checked Thomas with a glance. "Fight, did you say? No. You can have glorious arguments with Bronka, that's for sure, but not a cheap fight. I was out there for a few days that time because . . ." He drew noisily on his cigarette and spat a crumb of tobacco into the air.

"It won't work that way," said Crutches. "I have to begin this story sooner. How I got to know her. It was a while ago. It was in August 1944 in Breslau. Just before that, on July 20, General Claus von Stauffenberg led an assassination attempt on Hitler. But they failed to blow the Führer to kingdom come with their bomb. I was depressed that the attempt hadn't done much more than leave Hitler with a few scratches. Then they executed Stauffenberg and his cronies. I was part of a small group of students, most of us former soldiers who'd been turned into cripples, who decided to print fliers calling for an end to the war, to Hitler, to the Nazis. But the Gestapo were around everywhere and we were afraid we were being watched. We didn't circulate the fliers . . . out of fear, lack of courage."

With a powerful twist of his hand Crutches crushed the cigarette into the saucer.

"One of my friends," he continued, "took me into his confidence and asked for help. He and his wife had been hiding a young woman for a few weeks, a Jew. She couldn't stay with them any longer because his father-in-law was coming to visit, and he was a Nazi to the core. Could I do it, my friend asked."

Crutches thumped himself on the chest with his fist. "I still see myself standing there stupidly, hear myself stammering. Nothing but anxious, defensive thoughts chased through my head. What was he thinking of? How could I? Where could I put her? My friend observed my indecision and said I should think it over. I didn't do that. I just overrode my cowardice. I fetched her at night. She showed no trace of fear, she was such a bright, witty little bird. I won't tell you, Tom, what hidey-hole I found for her, how I learned to fear and hate dear neighbors. Just that, as so often in those days, the horrible became funny and the funny became horrible. At any rate, Bronka had got the idea in her head to get to Vienna. She knew two addresses there, and she'd be halfway safe. What else was there for me but to go along with her? I'll tell you, that was some undertaking. Sometimes I lost all belief that we'd ever get here. She never stopped believing. Never for a moment, I tell you. How do I know where she got the strength. Finally we reached Vienna, and the addresses were good. We got fantastic help. Bronka got papers, was properly registered with the authorities, and we moved into this apartment. Since then—oh yes, you wanted to know why I was staying out there in the country."

He leaned back and looked at the ceiling, as if he could read there what was so hard for him to say. "I don't know if you'll understand me, Tom. I don't want to deceive you. I love Bronka very much. She loves me, I'm sure. There is much that binds us together, perhaps too much. Often that's just what hurts. Especially when it becomes clear that eventually we must part. Sometimes I try it out. That's what that was."

"But—"

"No buts!" Crutches shook his head energetically. "Now both of us lazybones have to get up."

Another time Thomas began the lazy morning with a question that had bothered him for a long time. "Why don't I ever get to meet Bronka's children? What kind of children are they?"

Crutches turned over onto his side so that he could look at Thomas. "Even if you never see them face to face, my dear fellow, you know them. They are like you. At least who you are today. When you were a little Nazi, a pretty little wolf cub with a picture of Hitler in your head, they were dragged from their homelands to Germany along with their parents— children of foreign workers. Or, because they were Jews, they accompanied their mothers, their fathers,

their sisters to concentration camps—child prisoners." Crutches fell silent. He appeared to see children
in an endless line. Then he continued. "Many survived, but the mothers didn't. And the fathers didn't.
So now they are left, like you, on the railway platform. And there's an organization that concerns itself
primarily with Jewish orphans. Bronka works for
them, if one can call it work. She lives for the children
because she survived. And therefore I can hardly talk
her into taking you on, too. Clear?"

"Yes, Crutches." But really nothing was clear.
Much too much remained beyond his understanding.

Bronka routed them out of bed. "Now, this is really too much! You're sleeping away half your lives.
You're never going to get on in the world, Tom.
Crutches won't anyway. He's too lazy to get started."
She dug around in her large, bottomless handbag and
triumphantly waved a couple of papers in the air.
"Guess what I have for you." But she didn't give
them a chance to speak. "Travel permits for you
both! From the French military commission. You can
get a transport to Germany."

Crutches was silent and chewed on his lip.

Bronka let her arm fall. Her gray eyes darkened.
"Yes, I know, that means we only have five more
weeks together," she said softly.

Thomas felt a tightness in his chest—as he had that time on the platform when Mother disappeared.

Crutches pulled himself up. He hung between his crutches like a marionette on slack strings. Bronka was beside him in an instant. She didn't take him in her arms, just laid her head on his breast. And it was the old Crutches again who said, "Who's supposed to comfort whom, you ninny?"

◆

Leaving Bronka

Thomas began to count the days. The time flew.
Bronka had forbidden him and Crutches to speak of
their departure. But nevertheless parting hung over
them. They were restless and moody. There were no
more bed mornings. Crutches made his last rounds, as
he termed it, visited friends and acquaintances. Not
without a purpose. He intended to give Bronka a
beautiful piece of jewelry as a memento.

Doors opened to Crutches if he wanted them to.
He would be greeted in the center of the city with a
friendly murmur by the little groups of men who were
standing around.

"Do you know just about everyone here?"

"You know, Tom, here everyone cheats everyone
else and everyone deals with everyone. How you do

77

it is the only thing that matters. Above all, you mustn't consider the others stupider than you are. Then you can get along with almost everyone, except for the ones who have unrealistic ambitions. You're better off keeping out of their way."

In a café on the Ring they waited for a friend of Crutches'. Perhaps he could get them a beautiful ring or a bracelet. He specialized in those.

"And how will you pay for it?" asked Thomas.

Crutches scratched his neck, undecided, considering. "We'll work that out. Certainly not with new schillings. They're too expensive. Ah, here comes Poldi."

Crutches waved to a small, very smartly turned out man. Arms swinging, he wove his way between the tables, greeting people on all sides, giving the impression that the whole café belonged to him. Saying "Greetings," he sat himself down at their table, smiled at Crutches, swept Thomas with an inquiring glance, put his hand in his coat pocket, and pulled out a flat little black case.

"It seems you're in a hurry, Poldi?"

"You could say that." He opened the little case, holding his hand protectively over it.

Crutches shoved the hand slightly aside. "I'd like to be able to see your treasures."

And they were treasures! Golden rings in which stones sparkled and glowed, bracelets, and chains.

Poldi allowed them only a brief look. Sighing, as if he suffered under his occupation, he stuck the little box in his pocket, got up, and left without a farewell.

Amazed, Thomas looked after him. "Why did you let him go, Crutches? Those were beautiful rings."

Crutches laid his finger on his lips. "Speak softly, you donkey; it's nobody else's business."

He pulled himself up on his crutches, sighed somewhat the way Poldi had, and said, "I have to leave for a bit. Don't move from your place, and if anyone speaks to you, keep quiet."

Without hurrying, he hopped through the café and disappeared behind the door to the toilet.

Thomas didn't have to wait long.

Crutches returned, paid, and they left the café. After a few steps, Crutches stopped. "You want to see it?"

Like a magician he opened his clenched fist. In his hand lay a ring. He'd managed the deal in the short time he was outside.

"Just look at it," urged Crutches. "Put it on your finger, even if it won't fit."

The ring looked like a golden cord that was fastened together with a thick knot. In the knot, as if in a tiny crown, were a red stone and two clear ones. "The red one is a ruby," Crutches declared, "and the other two are diamonds."

"Bronka will really like this," said Thomas, and Crutches poked him happily in the side.

"That's just what I was going to ask you. Are you sure?"

"Yes, Crutches, especially because of the ruby."

Crutches wrapped the ring in a cloth and put it in his trouser pocket.

Bronka kept their spirits up. She took them out, and she even knew how to surprise Crutches. At the movies they saw a Russian film in which an indomitable hero conquered bears, ghosts, and an emaciated magician, and in a cellar club they listened to an audacious singer whose songs made fun of black marketeers, old Nazis, and new Austrians.

Bronka piled everything that she considered necessary for the journey in a corner of the bedroom. If the transport left on October 3 as planned, they would have to reckon with the onset of cold weather. Therefore she provided Tom with long trousers. He couldn't run around in his short pants forever.

Crutches grumbled about everything. Only the two quilts gained his approval. Because of them he was willing to take some unnecessary stuff along as part of the bargain. A person could be in trouble without blankets like that. He opened one out in the bedroom and said to Thomas, "Look, what do you see before you?"

Bewildered, Thomas answered, "What's it supposed to be, Crutches? A blanket, a quilt."

Crutches hopped around the blanket without stepping on it. "That's right, a blanket, and also a kind of room, a staked-out territory, which no one except you may lay claim to, on which you travel, eat, sleep, and in the worst case, die. Once you've spread the thing out somewhere, no one can take your place. Understand?"

Bronka, who was sitting on the edge of the bed, glanced up at Crutches with a smile. "There speaks the nomad from experience, Tom. Believe him. He is nothing, he has nothing, but still, that nothing has its boundaries. They are the edges of the blanket."

Sometimes Crutches stayed overnight with Bronka in the living room. Sometimes they decided to celebrate for no reason. Bronka invited Boris, David, and other friends in. All of them outtalked one another and outdid one another in telling stories about how they got away once again.

Crutches wanted to go to the Red Cross one last time to inquire for any news, and besides he wanted to report that he and Thomas were moving on.

He was soon back. "Nothing," he said, and he went to Thomas and took his face between his hands.

"She'll report. I'm sure of it. As soon as we arrive somewhere, we'll give the Search Office our new address. She can't fail you."

Crutches started to take his hands away, but Thomas held them fast and pressed them against his cheeks. Perhaps it didn't seem so important after all that Mama reported herself soon. Then what would happen to Crutches?

"And what will you do when we're gone, Bronka?"

"I'll miss both you crazies. Who will get me flour, dried eggs, and dried milk for my children when there's no more Crutches?" She cheered herself up. "Somebody will turn up. Some good soul has always appeared before. And sooner or later, Tom, I'm going to Palestine. That I know."

"Me too," said Crutches with a laugh. "I'll write you letters with the address 'Jerusalem' and drop in like a wild-bearded prophet."

"Are you sure that all prophets were bearded, Crutches?"

"What a question, Bronka, by the beard of the prophet!"

They're talking nonsense, Thomas thought, not to show how sad they are.

It was decided that Redlich would fetch them and

take them to the freight platform in Linzer Strasse.

"I can only hope he shows up without a trailer!"
Crutches mistrusted Redlich. But Redlich came not
only without a trailer, but without a car. Transformed into a coachman, Redlich was waiting for
them in front of the house in a beautiful old horse
cab.

Crutches looked over the horses and carriage and
blew his nose into a startlingly fresh handkerchief.
"Even if Vienna will scarcely remember us," he said,
"we're going to leave in style. No matter what!"
Which he underlined with another explosive blast
into the handkerchief.

Day broke hesitatingly and with the cold of autumn. Thomas shivered. It was less the cold that
gripped him than a great despondency. Wasn't it folly
to have joined Crutches? Mother would certainly
look for him in Vienna. And Bronka would certainly
keep him with her for a few more weeks.

The hoofbeats of the two horses multiplied in the
echo that bounced off the walls of the houses. There
were lights burning behind some windows. Thomas
sat between Bronka and Crutches and felt as gray
and miserable as the day.

"Is something wrong?" Bronka took his hand between hers and rubbed it.

"No."

"Really not?"

He would rather have howled, bellowed, stamped his feet, and let out his torturing uncertainty that way, but he only said softly, "No."

"Then it's all right."

Nothing's all right, he thought. Everything is mixed up. And I'm never going to get over it.

Crutches poked him with an elbow. "We're almost there, pal. We have to stick together. No one must separate us. Is that clear?"

Thomas nodded.

Crutches threw him a mistrustful glance. "Just don't get any howling miseries now, boy. That will only confuse things."

The cab turned off the street and drove along a steep alley to a kind of quay. There was no water flowing along it—but there was a railway track. The platform was packed with a limitless sea of people. Thomas couldn't imagine that they could all fit into one train.

"Are they all going with us?"

"It looks that way." Crutches rolled himself a cigarette with great speed. French soldiers ran around, dividing the crowd into small groups, counting, calling incomprehensibly to one another.

The train came in. An endless line of freight cars, on which large numbers had been written in chalk.

Redlich and Bronka pulled the bundles and knap-
sacks out of the cab. Crutches hung between his
sticks in frozen calm, the cigarette in the corner of his
mouth.

"They'll call us, Tom, together with the number of
the car we're assigned to. Then you grab both our
things, run there as fast as you can, get into the
boxcar, and spread out the quilts. In a corner, if you
get there in time."

"Yes, Crutches."

Bronka pressed him to her, kissed him on the
cheeks again and again. Her tears mixed with his.

"Keep your chin up, Tom, and keep an eye on
Crutches. You'll find your mama!"

Gently he freed himself from her embrace, said
good-bye to Redlich, who handed him a bar of chocolate, and picked up the bundled-up quilts. Crutches
should see right from the beginning that he was de-
pendable. He made his way between the people to the
podium on which two officers and a civilian were
standing. They held lists in their hands.

Just then they began to call out the names of the
travelers. "Kramer, Sybille, Car Five. Bertram,
Friedrich, and Bertram, Liese, Car Twelve."

Thomas closed his eyes and concentrated. He
never let go of the bundles. One name followed the
other. Maybe they forgot us, he thought. At that

moment he heard Crutches' voice as clear as a trumpet. "Eberhard Wimmer, that's me, Thomas! And son, that's you. Run, run, Car Seven!"

Thomas took off, bumped against people, received blows on his head, was shoved, was scolded, stumbled a few times over pieces of luggage, tore open his palms on the gravel ballast, dashed up to the chalked seven, threw both bundles into the freight car, made his way up hand over hand, shot to an empty corner, tore open the cords, spread the quilts out, and threw himself down on them, breathing hard. He had done it!

Not entirely. He first had to defend his borders. A young woman, without asking, just shoved one of the quilts aside, but she hadn't reckoned with his rage. "You. That's not allowed. Crutches is coming and you'll have to deal with him!"

And when two boys, not much older than he, settled down on the edges of the blankets, he kicked their backs, completely beside himself.

"Just get off. That's my blanket. Find your own place."

The boys grabbed him, and one began to pull his hair.

Crutches, hurry up and come, he thought. But he had to continue to battle a little longer. Suddenly a crutch was shoved between Thomas and the two boys. "Cut it out, you hollow-heads. And beat it,"

Crutches said. "Don't show your faces in this corner anytime soon. Is that clear?"

Pleased, Crutches regarded the island that Thomas had won. "Terrific," he said. He began to distribute the pieces of luggage so that finally there was just enough room for them both.

The train started with a jerk.

"Get yourself to the door and wave to Bronka. And for me too." Crutches lay down in the corner and closed his eyes. "For me too," he repeated.

The leave-takers crowded into the door of the freight car. Thomas crouched down and peered between their legs.

Bronka stood all alone. Redlich had made himself comfortable in the cab.

She stood there as if she'd forgotten something and was pondering over it. He couldn't wave to her. She would never have seen him anyway between all those legs. But he saw her. He thought, I love you, Bronka. And he thought, Why am I leaving?

The train clattered around a curve, and Bronka disappeared as if she'd been swallowed into the ground.

"Did you give her the ring?" he asked Crutches.

"Yes."

"Was she pleased?"

"And how."

T E N

Two Kinds of Duty

They'd been under way for three weeks. The train stopped more than it went. Every boxcar had forty passengers, some even a few more. People encroached on one another and tried to broaden their territories, to gain a bit more room to move. Sometimes this led to arguments.

For days Crutches had barely spoken at all; silently he would join Thomas in the line when the French army handed out stew and rations packets at the tiny railroad stations. All the same, Crutches had managed to get some women to give him the cigarettes out of their food packets. How he'd done this remained a riddle to Thomas.

It grew colder from day to day. Many were shivering and kept breaking into complaints about the terrible circumstances; the small children howled, when they weren't asleep from exhaustion.

The big sliding door stayed closed, although it stank horribly in the car. The dried marmalade was to blame for that. They'd found it in the rations packets along with the dried milk, zwieback, chocolate, and cigarettes. At first they didn't know what to do with the black tablets, until at some point a hungry person boldly bit off a piece of one and reported that it tasted good. In fact, the stuff didn't taste bad, if you chewed on it long enough. And it had an effect. People got diarrhea. Since the train command took no notice of the needs of individuals and the train couldn't keep stopping all the time, those who were hard pressed had to use a bucket for a latrine.

The cramped space led to quarrels, the stink led to quarrels. Everyone got on everyone else's nerves—this one kept coughing constantly, the other one snored, this brat kept bawling all the time, and that one was always sniffling, that slut never washed even in the stations, that old driveler had to spit on the floor. . . .

At first no one noticed the newcomer. He'd probably mixed in with the people at one of the stops. For a while he'd managed to avoid taking anyone's space and had pressed himself against the wall of the car.

Growing tired, he spread out and immediately met resistance.

"Where'd he come from all of a sudden?"

All at once everyone was awake and attentive. It was seldom enough that anything happened. Thomas sat up, but Crutches grasped his hand. "Keep out of it. Wait."

The newcomer had gotten up and was standing there with studied indifference. The curious made a circle around him, closing him in. He smiled, reached into the pocket of his army coat, from which the shoulder insignia had been removed, pulled out a handkerchief, took off his glasses, and began to polish them.

Every gesture proclaimed his calm and his superiority.

Rage rose in Thomas. He wanted to jump up, but Crutches wouldn't let go of him. "Don't mess with it," he murmured.

Thomas was only too familiar with fellows like that. Wherever he'd encountered them, in cellars or in train stations, everyone else had had to do what they said. Their parade-grounds voices brooked no argument. Even when everything was lost and the war was over.

Still this fellow remained silent, gave no orders. He waited.

Marie-Luise asked the first question. Thomas liked her. She didn't get excited over every tiny trifle and wasn't constantly scolding her two little boys; she even took care of the older people and played cards or guessing games with them.

She began carefully. "Have you mistaken the car number?"

The man put on his glasses again. "No, I haven't."

"But you can't do that, just board without asking."

"Why not? Whom should I ask? You?"

Thomas knew that tone. The man was going to put Marie-Luise in the wrong at the start. "Say something, Crutches," he whispered.

Crutches declined with a wave of his hand. "Let him go on a bit first."

"You don't need to ask me," said Marie-Luise. "You have to ask the transport command."

"Is there one?"

Marie-Luise looked around for help. Crutches drew up his leg. If only he would interefere, Thomas thought, but he was silent and remained sitting there.

One of the grandfathers grew brave. He asked the man to identify himself.

"Who are you to ask?" The voice of the intruder became a trace higher and sharper. "Who gave you the right?" He got no further.

"Stop!" Crutches had never gotten up onto his crutches so quickly. With a few swings he crossed the boxcar. Thomas followed him.

No one spoke. Even the children were quiet now. Only the thumping of the wheels was to be heard, and Crutches' breathing. Thomas pressed his fist against his mouth and chewed on his knuckles. He was afraid for Crutches.

"So, comrade, what's eating you?"

The man had inspected Crutches scornfully from head to toe, reproving him with glances. Now, astonished, he gasped. He hadn't reckoned on such an opening.

"And what is that supposed to mean?"

"You've been asked who you are, what your name is, and you've declined to give the information."

The man still could not take in Crutches' lack of respect. He straightened his glasses and was about to answer, but Crutches didn't give him a chance to. "A place like this is a first-class hiding place. One isn't likely to be detected among so many wretched people, right? Isn't that it?"

After a short pause, which Crutches savored, he added a prodding, interrogative "Or?"

"What if it is?" The stranger gave in but he didn't give up. "What have we done wrong? We've only done our duty. All at once that's not enough anymore. All at once we're hunted as criminals—officers of the German army!" He folded his arms tightly across his chest, as if to protect himself from persecutors.

Crutches straightened his leg, storklike, and made a tiny bow. "I also was an officer in the German army, comrade. But no one is hunting me. No one is persecuting me. I also don't know why. I take it we did two different kinds of duty. Yours was different from mine."

Until now the intruder had scarcely moved. Now he moved one step to the side so as not to face his opponent directly.

When he spoke, all the arrogance was gone from his voice. He no longer commanded, he entreated. "We're Germans; we should help one another in this terrible time of need. I beg you, take me in for a few days. As soon as the train comes to the German border, I'll leave."

"You will leave when the train stops the next time. Should you resist, we will all—children, women, cripples, and old people—join our strength and throw you out."

Why did Crutches have to carry it to excess? Why wouldn't he let the stranger talk? Thomas didn't understand this refusal. It hurt him. He pitied the intruder. So did the others.

"Why shouldn't he be able to stay for a few days?" asked a woman. "We only have to squeeze together a little, not much. And he hasn't done anything to us."

Blinking, Crutches looked into the depths of the boxcar. "No, he hasn't done anything to us. Not yet. We don't mean anything to him. He's using us, as he's used others. Consider what would happen if we were inspected today. What then? Then we've sheltered someone who's wanted for actual or suspected crimes. Then we're guilty too. And then our journey can end ahead of time."

Crutches didn't need to say anything more. The train stopped. The usual relief stop of ten minutes. Impatiently the door was thrown open. A cold wind blew into the car.

"Stop!" cried Crutches again. "Stop! He gets out first, and since, as I recall, German officers are courteous, he will also not keep us waiting long. Some of us have a pressing need to go behind the bushes." He nodded very seriously at the man. "Go! Don't force me to talk of manly courage and other virtues that you were championing so zealously a short time ago. . . . Please," he said once more.

Everyone stared at the man, waiting. A child said, "I have to peepee." Thomas could have wept. Probably Crutches was helping them. Still, this man who had given himself such airs in the beginning now seemed terribly destitute and alone. They watched—some sighed—as the stranger squeezed himself along the wall in small steps, reached the door, hesitated once more, and finally jumped down onto the embankment. He went without looking back.

They relieved themselves.

When the locomotive whistled, they all silently found their places again, communing with themselves.

Thomas pressed against Crutches and, when the tears came to his eyes, laid his head on his chest.

Crutches spoke softly to him. "It's bad, Tom, when wrong is repaid with wrong. I didn't begin it. I wish I could change it. Probably he was an SS officer and is on a wanted list. In many cases these men have shown no mercy. They've ordered murders and have themselves murdered. Think of Bronka! She might have been one of his victims. No, I'm not going to play judge. Probably he'll get away. These lads are very good at surviving. Probably you'll meet him again someday—as a factory director or in an office, and he won't remember a thing anymore. But I'm not going to think that far."

Crutches pulled Thomas closer to him. "Go to sleep," he said. "And if you can, don't dream."

At the Border
but Not Home Yet

The mood in Car 7 sank to zero—like the temperature outside. Nearly all the children had fevers and were wrapped like mummies in coats and blankets. One of the old men, Grandpa Bednarz, lay dying. Nobody knew, not even the transport command, when or where the train would arrive. It was traveling in a circle, it was said; no place in Germany wanted to take in the refugees.

Crutches comforted and calmed, cracked jokes, played with the children, and invented stories in which he himself always played the clown. Since the set-to with the stranger, he was respected in the boxcar.

At the end of the fifth week, Grandpa Bednarz died. His wife and the other women had taken turns caring for him.

Someone said, "Grandpa Bednarz is dead."

He'd traveled with them, and now he wasn't there anymore. Thomas heard Frau Bednarz sobbing. He put his hands over his face and peered through the cracks between his fingers over to where the old man lay on a mattress. He was afraid of the dead man and yet he regarded him curiously.

Crutches sensed his uneasiness. "Come," he said, "we'll go say good-bye to old Bednarz."

He's asleep, thought Thomas, he's asleep without breathing. No wrinkles in the face moved, and the eyelids remained closed, without fluttering.

"May it go well with you, old fellow, wherever you are," Crutches murmured.

At the next stop, Grandpa Bednarz was removed from the car.

His wife refused to travel farther. "He'll be buried here," she said, "and I'll stay with him. Maybe it will be a little corner of heaven."

"What's this dump called, anyway?" someone asked.

"Waldkirchen am Wesen."

"Then it's not far to Passau and to the border," one of the women chimed in. "I know that for sure. I know the region."

This statement worked like a magic charm, changing the people and the atmosphere with one stroke.

People were seized with excitement. Everything that had tormented and depressed them was forgotten— the cold, the uncertainty, the illness, old Bednarz.

The border!

The train started again, and they didn't even notice. In their thoughts they hurried it forward. At last there was a goal. At last they were no longer traveling around without purpose.

As if obeying an unspoken order, many people began to arrange their luggage. Some looked in their pockets for their papers. Women combed their children's hair, as if they had to look especially nice at the border.

Crutches, too, became fidgety.

"Sit down," he said imperiously to Thomas.

"But I am sitting down."

"I mean move a bit closer to me."

"Why?"

Angrily Crutches grabbed his arm. "Don't ask. Do as I tell you."

Thomas looked at him in alarm. So far nothing on the long journey had managed to shake Crutches' calm. All at once he was going crazy. The border couldn't be that important.

"They will probably interrogate us, do you understand?"

"Why?"

"You're asking that again!" Crutches rolled his eyes and blew out his cheeks as if he were about to explode. "Dear Lord, how can a person be so dense!" To calm himself, he spoke with exaggerated softness and distinctness. "You have no papers, Tom. You cannot identify yourself. I must vouch for you. I must declare why we are together. Clear?"

"Yes." But still he considered Crutches' excitement overreacting. He hadn't been asked for identification anywhere during his wanderings. He had none at all. Mother had sometimes mentioned that he was entered in her papers.

"To be prepared for all eventualities, we need to talk over once more what we might be asked. We must not contradict each other. Otherwise they'll get suspicious and . . . ." Crutches took a deep breath. "That's not to be thought of! So pay attention. I am your uncle, married to the sister of your mother. We met by chance in Vienna, where we were both looking for Aunt Wanda. How you lost your mother at the station in Kolin, how you made your way to Vienna, all that you can tell truthfully, as it happened. My name is Eberhard Wimmer." Crutches held up his hand and at each name he bent a finger.

Thomas tried to imitate him. As easy as it looked, he didn't succeed.

"Keep your mind on it. Your name is Thomas

Schramm. Your father was Ferdinand Schramm. Your mother's name is Erika and she was born Ziedler. Is that right?"

Thomas found nothing in Crutches' recital to disagree with. "Yes."

Broodingly, Crutches regarded his hand with its bent fingers. Apparently he considered the mutual examination at an end, for he let his arm fall and leaned against the wall of the boxcar. "Later on— there's no hurry—we should put our worldly goods in order. Who knows how long we'll be allowed to stay in this parlor car."

Thomas breathed a sigh of relief. Crutches had his sense of humor back.

Some of the passengers who were especially impatient had shoved the door open a crack, had peered out, and were telling people in the car what they saw. "We're going along a river. Quite a narrow valley. It's probably the Danube."

A hectic joy spread among the passengers. The sick children no longer wanted to lie quietly, and the women remonstrated with them. Old men told how they had experienced the Danube in earlier days. In Vienna, in Melk, in Passau. In summer, along with a lady friend. In spring, when the floodwaters overflowed the banks. The Danube was right up to the middle of the car, at least in their stories.

When the train finally came to a halt and loud
voices were heard outside, the people were sitting or
lying in their regular places, exhausted. The door was
thrown open and two men in civilian clothes looked
over the inhabitants as if they were merely crates or
barrels to be dealt with. One of them paged through
a notebook, the other picked his nose. Both seemed
tired and indifferent. Probably, thought Thomas,
we're all the same to them, and they won't ask us
much at all.

"Car Seven. Forty-three people," stated one.

The other took his finger out of his nose and repeated the count, whereupon Crutches said in the
same tone of voice. "Car Seven, forty-one people."

That was too much for the two of them. With open
mouths they stared into the freight car. "What's
that? Who was that?"

Crutches pulled himself up and hopped to the
door.

"I. We are forty-one. Two people have left us."

"Left?" the man asked, as if Crutches were talking
a foreign language.

"Yes, left."

"Did they at least report to the transport command?"

Crutches hung between the sticks like a question
mark and took time with his answer. "Now you em-

barrass me. That's not so easy to answer. Shall we say, Grandpa Bednarz, no; Grandma Bednarz, under pressure of necessity."

"You're a regular joker, aren't you? You're just wasting our time. We have to deal with two transports a day here. Can you imagine what that means? So, now, what's the story with these two slobs who're missing?"

He said "slobs." With this word he struck out and hit them all. It was an angry, icy word.

"Now, now," the people inside the boxcar murmured.

Crutches straightened up, stood stiff and unwavering on his one leg, and looked over the men's heads toward a rambling series of sheds. "Since you place such value on precision, I also will be precise. Grandpa Bednarz died. His wife wanted to remain with him."

It was a kind of angry obituary notice. Thomas recollected how Grandpa Bednarz had been lifted out of the boxcar and placed on the baggage cart instead of suitcases and boxes. Two station attendants had pulled him along the length of the train. Grandma Bednarz had walked behind him, a suitcase in each hand, utterly alone.

"All in order." The man folded the list and shoved it into his pocket.

The border people had had plenty of practice. The people were dispatched with a speed that took their breath away. Their names were called over a loudspeaker. Then they hurried through a slalom in which they were disinfected, examined, interrogated, and validated. Thomas, fearful of becoming separated from Crutches, stuck close behind him.

At the first station they were dusted. "Men and women separately. Move along, move along, step lively!" They were ordered to uncover their upper bodies, open their trousers. Then they moved in a comical line, step by step, trousers slipping, up to two men in white coats, who used an apparatus like a vacuum cleaner that didn't suck in dust but sprayed it out in a thick vapor. "It isn't dangerous," the men with the dust gun said reassuringly. "The dust is for lice, bugs, and scabies."

Some laughed when the dust stream went into their trousers. Crutches told them not to fill his empty trouser leg with the damned stuff. Thomas had decided to endure the procedure quietly, but when the dust stream touched him, he jumped from one leg to the other, giggling, until Crutches poked him in the back. "This really isn't that funny."

A doctor awaited them at the second station. He asked each person to open his mouth as wide as possible. He looked inside, nodded, and thanked them.

"Do you know what he was looking for?" asked Thomas on the way to the third station.

"How should I know that!" Crutches spat so hard that he seemed to be trying to rid himself of what the doctor had seen. "Why didn't you ask the doctor himself? Probably he wanted to see our souls."

"You can't see those, Crutches."

"Maybe *he* could."

At the end of the rambling shed, which smelled of hay and horses, the line of people coiled itself before a barrier of tables.

Thomas found time to look around him and discovered that the room was divided by a partition the height of a man, and the line wound itself behind it. Everyone spoke softly, so there was an uninterrupted murmur overall. There were soldiers widely spaced, leaning against the wall. They had to see to it that people stayed in line, Thomas supposed. To his astonishment they weren't French but American. He plucked Crutches' sleeve. "Hey, those are Amis!"

Crutches didn't get excited. "They're all exactly the same," he said. "The important thing is for them to let us through without any trouble."

At the tables up ahead there were questionnaires that had to be filled out. "That's all we needed." Crutches became uneasy and busied himself with lighting a cigarette.

All kinds of silly ideas streamed through Thomas's head. Perhaps I'll begin to sing, he thought, and distract them that way.

Finally they were there. Crutches read through the paper and sighed with relief. "You don't have to fill it out. I have to declare if there are children under fourteen in my care. Everything's all right, pal!"

He sank onto a stool and Thomas just managed to catch the crutches. Crutches began to write. Curiously Thomas peered over his shoulder. Obviously the questionnaire hadn't been made up for Crutches. Member of the National Socialist Party? No! Member of the SS? No!

In return for the completed questionnaire they received not one but two documents. Travel passes, the older woman behind the desk called them.

"Now that's something!" Crutches snorted like a sounding whale. "For the first time you are in possession of some papers!" He gave Thomas a paper. "Hold on to it, my boy, and don't let anything eat it up."

The last examination was quickly behind them. Passes were stamped. Everyone got a food packet. Finally their names were crossed off still another list.

"So nobody can get lost," Crutches said.

One after the other they clambered back into Car 7. They all brought rumors with them:

The transport would go on this evening.

No, they had to change trains.

Probably they were going to Bavaria.

That was crazy. It was said that Thuringia was their destination.

Crutches listened, shaking his head. Finally he'd had enough. "Well, I wouldn't break my head over any of that. Probably they don't have any more idea than we do, and we'll be circling around from platform to platform for a while longer!"

One of the rumors was true. The train did move on that evening.

When they settled down for the night, they discovered that someone was missing. "Herr Bohmer isn't here! And all his things are going on with us."

"They held him."

"Probably he had some dirt in his record."

"Someone was pulled out of line in front of us, too."

"But Bohmer! He was always so nice and polite."

Why, Thomas mused, couldn't you tell by looking at someone who he was and what he had done? Tired, he wrapped himself in his blanket and closed his eyes.

"Comfortable, Tom?" he heard Crutches ask before Car 7 shook him to sleep.

◆

Light Behind a Window

The transport stopped in Landshut. The locomotive disappeared into the broad, endless landscape of tracks. Even to those who never gave up hope, it was clear that they must reckon with a period of more waiting, forgotten in a wasteland, fed with hopes by the transport escort, who probably knew just as little about it as they did.

Crutches found this not very remarkable. "Consider how many trains just like ours there are now, Tom. From east to west, from north to south. Filled with people who want to arrive somewhere. But that somewhere doesn't even have a name. It's quite possible that a train might be forgotten, disappear from the travel plan that was so hastily arranged, and sit forever on some siding."

"And then?" Thomas resisted Crutches' black picture.

"And then?" Crutches acted astonished. "Can't you imagine what would happen then? One person after the other would leave the train, go across the tracks into the city to look for a place to stay, to look for work, or to go on—those who might put up with being provided with soup from the Red Cross once a day and freezing like a tailor at night. Down to those who will stay, the discouraged, the weary. Sometime someone will discover them and marvel at them, the way they did at the cavemen. Perhaps people will speak of them as 'boxcar men.' "

"Will we be like that?"

"No," said Crutches. "Certainly not. You can bet on it." He pointed out toward the tracks with his crutch. "In your place I wouldn't just sit around here but would go out and explore the territory a little."

How many stations, freight platforms, empty railroad tracks Thomas had gotten to know lately! It had long since ceased to be difficult for him to walk on gravel ballast or ties. If the stations had not been bombed, usually the waiting rooms would be heated, and he could get warm there until the railroad clerks asked to see tickets and chased out uninvited guests.

Thomas tiptoed carefully across the tracks. This

station had been utterly destroyed by bombs. He had to watch out for the craters in which black, oily-looking water had collected. Some tracks were already repaired, and the rails that had been twisted by explosions lay beside them. Other rails just bent up into emptiness.

In a shed he discovered a handcar. It was standing behind the half-open door as if it were waiting for him. He climbed up onto the platform and leaned on the drive lever, trying to push it down and set the handcar in motion. The lever wouldn't move. He didn't care. He only needed to close his eyes and the handcar moved, rolled silently, faster and faster; all signals were raised as if by magic, signaling clear tracks. Alongside the tracks people were waving. It got warmer and brighter. He had left winter behind him and was riding into summer.

Voices snatched him out of his dream. Two railroad workers had come into the shed. Apparently they hadn't discovered him yet. They were talking and kept standing where they were. He ducked, sprang from the handcar, and tried to slip out the door unnoticed. He didn't succeed.

"Damn it all," swore one man. "This rabble is running all over everywhere." The other reached for a piece of ballast stone and threw it at Thomas.

Thomas ran, stumbled over the sliding stones, hopped over tracks. He was determined they wouldn't catch him, no matter what. He didn't look around, heard only his own breathing.

Finally he stopped and looked back. The two men hadn't moved from the spot, only watched his flight. It annoyed him that he'd given in to his fear.

Far off stood the transport, as small as a toy train.

What would Crutches do if the train left and I wasn't back, he wondered.

He laughed to himself.

Probably Crutches would try to stop the train with screaming and threats. But he certainly wouldn't come looking for him. Crutches didn't like hopping along the sliding ballast on his crutches.

A little wall now separated Thomas from a street and a shabby residential area. Still breathing hard, he climbed onto the wall and made himself comfortable.

The railroad workers had disappeared into the shed. He wanted to wait until they left the area. If they caught him, it could cause difficulties with the transport command.

He lay on his back, though he could feel the cold stone through his jacket, and crossed his hands behind his neck. He had time. Soon it would be dark.

At the horizon, where the city must be, the sky

turned yellow—a depressing, unfriendly sky. Billows of black cloud hung so low that they nearly grazed the roofs of the houses.

Now and again Thomas looked over at the shed.

The men seemed to have been busy for a long time.

He got cold. He sat up, pulled his knees to his chest, and dozed. It began to get dark. In front of him, in one of the houses opposite, a light went on in a window. The bright cutout in the dusk pulled him into a strange undertow. He wanted to be in that room—sitting around the table with Mama, with Crutches and Bronka, not freezing outside as he was.

Spellbound, he gazed at the bright spot. He felt envious of everyone who could be in such a light in a room, who was at home. Then a wave of defiance and rage seized him, and he was close to throwing a stone at the light, to punish these people who had everything, who didn't care about anything, who retreated behind the window into warmth, into security.

He jumped down from the wall and walked slowly across the tracks to the transport. Now he no longer feared the railroad workers. They were among those who could retreat into warm rooms. If they caught him, he would be silent and scorn them. And they would have to be ashamed.

But when he came to the shed, it was quiet. The workers must have left while he was staring at the window.

Step by step he neared the boxcar. It was after all a kind of home. Fires burned in front of some of the cars, throwing flames high, and people stood around them in a tight circle. On each car hung an oil lantern. Together the long string created a flickering garland.

Crutches scarcely looked up when Thomas sat down beside him. "You were away for a pretty long time."

"Yes."

"And what did you find out?"

"There's a handcar over there in the shed."

"Did you want to take off with it?"

"No. It wouldn't go, anyway."

"And was that all?"

"Yes."

"Then we'll have supper now." Crutches pulled the bread out of the ration box, cut off four slices, laid two in front of Thomas, two beside himself, and said, "After your exertions I'll allow us some more margarine and a respectable dollop of mustard."

T H I R T E E N
The Guardian

The transport had traveled back and forth for six long weeks before it reached a destination. At least a provisional one. They were housed in a camp at the edge of the Schwabian city of Wasseralfingen; from there they were supposed to be parceled out later among the cities and villages in the countryside.

At last they stood on firm ground. At last the floor no longer rattled beneath them. At last the days were no longer divided according to when and where the train stopped. The travelers were so exhausted they could hardly take pleasure in it.

Instructed ahead of time by Crutches, Thomas won them a double-decker bed at the end of a long row of beds in one of the barracks. Each building had places for about eighty people. Crutches settled himself in the bottom bunk, Thomas in the top one.

In the aisle between the beds, which were placed against the walls, stood long tables and benches. For a few days there were squabbles over places. At their table Crutches had seen to it that people quickly came to an agreement. The noise in the long room was often very loud. The people bellowed, scolded, and complained; there were always children crying somewhere.

But there were amenities that Thomas had almost forgotten. They had hot meals regularly. They could shower in the bath barracks, after they stood in line for a while.

Thomas joined a group of children who were already well known in the camp and in the surrounding area. Diethelm, the leader, had come from the Riesengebirge, so they called themselves the Ruebezahl gang after the giant-hero of the local folktales.

They didn't just roam around; they worked to make sure that the barracks were properly warm.

The daily allotment of firewood for the cast-iron stove was never enough. It was difficult to get hold of enough wood. The fruit orchards in the vicinity of the camp were watched by the farmers. If the farmers caught one of the children, the "supervisory personnel" got into trouble with the camp command; besides, the culprit had to reckon with a sound thrashing. So the Ruebezahl gang combed the forests. Even that wasn't without danger. They weren't the only ones looking for wood, pinecones, or beech brush. Their finds were often disputed by grown-ups. Sometimes the constables or the foresters even chased them. So it could happen that they returned without anything, and the people in the barracks froze.

One morning Crutches refused to leave his bed. His looks frightened Thomas. His forehead was covered with beads of sweat, his eyes were sunk in deep hollows, and his beard stubble was so dark that it looked as though he hadn't shaved in days. He seemed to have a weight on his chest. He spoke with effort and haltingly.

"Just leave me alone, Tom. Don't talk to me, don't ask me anything, don't get on my nerves. I ache in three legs and two heads."

He groaned and gasped for breath.

"This damn malaria. I was hoping that it would hold off for a while longer."

Again he struggled for air.

"The only loot I brought home from Russia."

"Can I do anything for you?"

"Yes, give me your blanket. I'm freezing like a tailor."

This was a Crutches that Thomas didn't know. A helpless man who let himself be cared for without argument.

"Shall I run over to the medical barracks?"

"Wait a while yet!"

Crutches seemed to shrink under the doubled blankets. His whole body began to shake and his teeth chattered.

Thomas was alarmed. Crutches didn't react at all when he stood up and hurried away from the bed.

He ran along the aisle between the beds and crossed the courtyard, talking out loud to himself. "Crutches is sick, terribly sick, he has malaria, he has fever. Crutches can't die. He can't die!"

A man was blocking the door of the medical barracks. Thomas tried to duck past but the man grabbed him by the arm. It hurt.

"Where are you going?"

"To the doctor."

"Something the matter with you?"

Without changing expression, the man twisted Thomas's arm behind his back. Thomas screamed out with pain.

"I asked you if something was the matter with you."

"No." He wasn't able to repress a groan.

"Sure?"

"No." He ought to have kicked the man or called for help. He did nothing, just let himself be tortured by this fellow.

"My uncle," he said.

The man laughed. "Well, well, your uncle—"

He got no further. The door opened. A Red Cross nurse looked out inquiringly.

The man let go of Thomas, nodded to the nurse, and went away as if nothing had happened.

The nurse looked after him mistrustfully. "A nasty fellow," she said. Then she turned to Thomas. "What did he do to you?"

"Nothing. It wasn't bad. But Crutches," he said. "Crutches has malaria."

"Crutches?"

That stupid name, which he liked and no one else ever understood. "My uncle," he corrected himself. "I have to get the doctor."

"He isn't here. Come in." She went ahead of him.

It smelled of medicine in the corridor. He heard her murmur, "Malaria?" as if she had just now grasped his message. She turned around at the word and laid her hand on his shoulder, which still hurt from the bully's grip.

"We'd better look at your sick uncle right now. What's your name?"

"Thomas."

"Take me to him, Thomas."

The visit turned out to be brief. She looked at Crutches. He was asleep. He seemed to be tormented by bad dreams. He groaned, rolling his head back and forth. Sometimes when he exhaled, little bubbles of saliva frothed between his lips.

"The doctor will come right over," she promised. And she was gone.

Soon the doctor arrived. Not alone, but accompanied by two ambulance attendants, who carefully lifted Crutches from the bed and onto a stretcher.

Thomas looked on, beside himself. What was happening could not be true. He was dreaming. He was dreaming that Crutches was being carried out of the barracks, that the doctor declared, "The man must go to the hospital in Aalen." He was dreaming that he heard himself screaming. He was dreaming that he ran into a trap of many arms, which embraced him and held him fast, that these arms pressed him onto the bed and someone talked incomprehensibly to him.

"Doesn't the boy have anyone?" he heard a strange voice say.

"No," it screamed in his head.

"He has to calm down first," said the strange voice. As if over a loudspeaker. A hand grasped his face. He pressed his eyelids shut, refused to open his eyes. He must not see that what he had seen was true. The hand pressed his cheeks, forcing him to open his mouth. Bitter juice ran onto his gums. He swallowed, heard himself swallowing. Still the arms pressed him down on the bed, then gradually he became lighter; he had the feeling he was flying or falling.

He emerged from deep sleep unwillingly. His first thought was, Crutches! Where did they say he was supposed to be? The first word that he spoke aloud was the same. "Crutches!"

To which he received a remarkable answer. "Man, oh man!" He blinked.

Flanked by his friends from the Ruebezahl gang, Diethelm sat on the edge of the bed and observed his awakening intently.

"Man, oh man, did you sleep a long time! Like dead, I can tell you. We thought they gave you an overdose. But Nurse Monika said no. One night and half a day! Lunch is already over. But"—Diethelm let his voice drop—"we kept out your share. D'you want to eat now?"

"No, not really. What about Crutches?"

His question had a remarkable effect. As if at a signal, all the Ruebezahlers placed themselves around his bed, a living fence that closed him in and protected him.

Out of his pants pocket Diethelm pulled a piece of paper, folded very small. "It's from Crutches. Nurse Monika brought it and gave it to us because we're your friends." He gave the note to Thomas.

Thomas folded it into his fist.

"We haven't read it, I swear," Diethelm reassured him.

They told him Crutches wasn't the first one from the camp who'd been taken to the hospital at Aalen. He could visit soon. And Nurse Monika would come and get him tomorrow because she wanted to talk with him some more about everything. She'd said so.

They stood around him eagerly and expectantly. But he could only think of Crutches' note. He wanted to read it alone, undisturbed.

"You guys are great," he said. "Thanks."

The whole gang beamed. They all began talking at once again. As long as Crutches was in the hospital, they'd divide the work. Half the gang would take care of wood, the other half would take care of Thomas. It was all set.

"Great," said Thomas. Crutches' message burned in his hand. "Could you . . . Now could I—"

"I know," Diethelm interrupted him. "You want

to read Crutches' note." Thomas nodded. The friends streamed off in a line, with Diethelm at the head.

It wasn't easy to unfold the note. "My writing is a little wobbly from malaria," he read. "I hope you can decipher it, Tom boy. Don't worry. This isn't my first attack. In a few days I'll be over the hump. Maybe you can come visit me, pal. Keep your chin up and keep my bed free. Your old Uncle Crutches."

He heard Crutches' voice. Each word cheered him. He took a deep breath and felt like running outdoors. He dressed hurriedly, which did not escape Diethelm's notice. When he walked out of the barracks and sucked in the cold air, his bodyguard surrounded him. He liked that. No one would be able to do anything to him.

Next morning Nurse Monika caught him in the courtyard. He could come right now. She had to ask him some questions.

"Now?" Why couldn't even such a friendly and helpful person as Nurse Monika leave him alone?

"Yes, then we'll have it behind us."

"Will it take long?"

"No."

He trotted along beside her, asked himself if he should run away, and decided not to; he didn't want to do anything that would look suspicious.

In her narrow little office behind a partition, into which a table, two chairs, and a filing cabinet had been shoehorned, it smelled wonderfully of apples. They lay in a dish on the table.

"Take one and sit down."

He hadn't bitten into an apple in an eternity. He chewed greedily and nearly choked.

Strangely serious, Nurse Monika regarded him. "They're from our garden. You can take a few with you afterward if you like."

His "Thank you" was scarcely intelligible through the crunching.

Finally she smiled. "Be careful, Thomas!"

As if preparing for a hearing, she arranged papers on her desk.

"It has to do with the following." Again she stopped, laid one of the papers to one side. "We've discovered in the lists from the Red Cross that you are looking for your mother. Is that so?"

"Yes." He swallowed down the last piece of apple.

"You've given as your address one in Vienna. Did you live there with Crutches, I mean with Herr Wimmer?"

Why did she speak so impersonally of Crutches, calling him Herr Wimmer? Was that by design? Did she want to trap him?

"Yes, with Bronka."

"And who is that?"

How should he explain that to her? He decided to be as brief as possible. "A friend of Crutches'. And of mine too."

She seemed content with that. "Have you heard anything about your mother meanwhile?"

"No." Becoming careful, he added, "We asked at the Red Cross a couple of times and also notified them when we left Vienna. Until we have a place to stay somewhere, Bronka will get our mail."

"And your father?"

"He was killed in action."

"And Crutches?" Nurse Monika folded her hands and bent forward slightly. "It's all right for me to call him Crutches, isn't it?"

"Of course."

"Are you related to him?"

Without his realizing it, she'd cornered him. He couldn't simply lie. She'd know.

He became red and got muddled. Hesitantly he began, "I've been with him for a long time. A very long time," he insisted. "He took care of me. Because I'm alone, until we've found Mama." He stared at her hands, with which she had helped him and at the same time had complicated things for him.

"I asked you something, Thomas. You still haven't answered me."

"Yes?"

"Are you related to Crutches?" she insisted.

He looked out the window. It was snowing for the first time this year.

"It's snowing," he said softly.

She turned around briefly but turned right back to him.

"He's my uncle." He thought of Crutches' letter and how he had signed it *Uncle Crutches.*

"That's what you call him?"

"Yes. Uncle Crutches. Mostly I just call him Crutches."

"He's not your real uncle, is he?"

Why was she tormenting him? What did she have against him and Crutches?

"Yes, he is," he said defiantly. Even if Nurse Monika thought he was a liar, from this moment on Crutches was his real uncle and would remain so forever.

She pushed herself away from the desk with both hands, stood up sighing, went to the filing cabinet, took out a folder, and leafed through it.

Thomas waited with head lowered.

"Did you go with him voluntarily?"

"I don't understand. Of course."

She stood behind him. Her nearness made him uncomfortable. He hunched his shoulders.

"You met and talked with each other. It's quite imaginable that he persuaded you to go with him in some way. For some reason or other."

She's imagining things, he thought. She has no idea at all. He shook his head vigorously. "No. I wanted to. I love Crutches. He is my uncle. That's true."

"And did he get you to look for your mother?"

"Yes."

She returned to her seat and looked him in the eyes. "Does Crutches know your mother?"

"No," he said, and he could have torn himself to pieces with rage.

"Now that's really funny. If he is, as it says here, married to your mother's sister, he must know her."

"Yes," he said and pressed his lips together. The dumb goose could think what she wanted to. He'd made a bad mistake, she'd led him into it. That wouldn't happen to him again.

Now she spoke over his head, as if it had nothing to do with him. "We have instructions to report orphaned children or children who come to us in the camp without parents or relatives. A guardian must be appointed for them, someone to speak up for them. Do you understand? That must also be done for you."

"No!" He forced himself to remain sitting there, not to run away. She must not see his fear. He pressed his legs together, but his hands moved independently of his wishes and rubbed the edge of the desk like crazy. "Crutches is my uncle. I don't need all that, and no guardian either."

"Good," said Nurse Monika. "As long as Crutches is in the hospital, we'll put you in Barracks Three. You'll be better taken care of there. And you'll find children who've had experiences similar to yours. Besides, there are three nurses to take care of you."

"No!" Now it didn't matter. Now he could clear out. He jumped up and she looked at him, astonished. He shook his head, tore open the door, and ran out.

Snowflakes wafted against his face, melted on his skin, and mixed with tears. "If only Crutches would come," he kept saying to himself.

Diethelm and the Ruebezahl gang took charge of him in the courtyard. He didn't have to say much.

"They want to stick me in some crummy children's barracks. That just can't be true."

Thomas entrenched himself in his top bunk. Diethelm and the Ruebezahlers succeeded in alerting the whole barracks in a very short time. People whom

Thomas knew only by sight came to him, patted him gently. He shouldn't get excited. He would stay with them until Crutches was back from the hospital and the matter could be settled. Before that nothing would happen to him. They would all see to that.

They kept their promise.

When Nurse Monika and the camp director appeared and began to make their way to Thomas's bed, grown-ups and children stood in their path, with the Ruebezahl gang in front. Thomas pulled the blanket up to his nose and lay stiff as a board.

"We want to get to Thomas," he heard Nurse Monika say.

A man's voice answered, quietly and firmly. "I know. You want to change his quarters. You mustn't do that. All of us here will take care of him as long as Crutches has to stay in the hospital."

"Yes?" said Nurse Monika. Her voice sounded doubtful.

Since no one said anything more, Thomas sat up and caught sight of the camp director closing the door behind him. A miracle had occurred.

Diethelm threw up his arms and bellowed, "We did it!"

"Do you know who it was who spoke up for me so strongly?" Thomas asked Diethelm.

"I certainly do," Diethelm boasted proudly. "That was my grandpa. A great old guy, isn't he?"

Three days later Thomas was allowed to visit Crutches in the hospital. Nurse Monika accompanied him. He'd refused to go anywhere near her, but Diethelm's grandfather had talked him out of it. "She can't do anything to us. We know what's what."

The doctor took them in his car. Nurse Monika said that she'd talked with Crutches a few times. He was doing very well indeed, astonishingly well, after that severe attack.

The doctor parked the car in front of a burned-out house, and they reached the hospital along a path between two collapsed walls.

Crutches sat up in bed expectantly. His head seemed smaller, even more birdlike; his chest looked thin and sunken.

Thomas saw something that until now he had considered utterly impossible. Crutches was crying. Thomas cried too.

Nurse Monika and the doctor swiftly left the sickroom. The patients in the other beds acted as if Thomas and Crutches weren't there.

Crutches hugged him. He smelled different. Not like tobacco, sweat, or shaving soap, but awfully clean. Thomas clung to Crutches and thought, Now

Nurse Monika can't do anything more against us. Nothing.

Gently Crutches pushed him away and wiped his face with his handkerchief.

"Us two crybabies," he said. "This is too much." He laughed drily. "God in Heaven, what I wouldn't give for a cigarette! But smoking's not allowed here."

He surveyed Thomas. "We haven't much time, Tom. What I have to say to you now is important. Yesterday I gave a full account to Nurse Monika. She told me about you. You behaved wonderfully, boy. But I didn't keep anything back from her. She knows everything now. We can stay together until you've found your mother again. Now we only have to report when we find out where we'll be living, so that someone who can speak up for you, a guardian, can be appointed for you. It might even be me."

"You?"

Crutches smiled. The lines in his face crinkled.

"You've struck it lucky. You're going to have a bigmouth to speak up for you."

They laughed so hard that Nurse Monika looked in curiously through the door.

"It's time," she warned. "Come on, Thomas, say good-bye to Crutches. And you and I can make peace now, I think."

♦

On the Way to Bethlehem

The Ruebezahl gang melted away to only a few members. Nearly every day large groups left the camp for the railroad station. This time they knew where they were going, where they would probably find a home. Nevertheless, the barracks filled up as fast as they emptied. New trains arrived constantly. Every Ruebezahler was seen off with full ceremonies. Before the train left, they swore not to forget one another and to write as soon as they had new addresses. After Diethelm and his family had left, the remaining Ruebezahlers elected Thomas captain. But he soon lost his momentum. He lacked the energy and the good humor. He preferred to climb back up to his perch in the upper bunk and daydream and brood and discuss with Crutches where they might finally end up.

They invented lots of place names with the *-ingen* ending that was so common in Schwabia and tried to outdo each other in wild wordplay.

"Overunderingen!"

"No, Spilloverthingen."

"What do you think of Smallingen?"

"I like Biglingen better."

"Or Nowhereingen."

Crutches sighed. "That's probably where we'll end up."

He'd been playing cards with himself lately, solitaire. "I just get into arguments with the other poker players around here," he said. "Because I know a few more tricks. I cheat, they say."

Now and then Nurse Monika would check up on them. When she had time, she went for a walk with Crutches. Thomas was certain that she was in love with Crutches. He said as much to him, too. "You, I think you've fallen head over heels!"

Crutches denied it. "No, Tom, that's just my nurse technique. I got it during my long stay in the field hospital. As soon as a starched cap shows up, I automatically begin with the sweet talk. Not because I was a flirt to start with—quite the contrary! No, there are a lot of dragons among them, and I learned to tame them this way."

Although the stove in the barracks glowed, it was

barely warm. The older camp inhabitants almost never left their beds anymore.

The camp authorities provided warm clothing from the stores of the former Winter Help Program.

Crutches exchanged his bizarre jacket for a much-too-large knuckle-length coat that sported a mangy fur collar. He paraded enthusiastically in front of Thomas, turned, and slapped the dust out of the material.

"It's hard to believe," he said, "but the madness of our Adolf, the greatest general of all time, did have just a little method. What never reached us in Russia is now handed out to us in peaceful Wasseralfingen. Strategy, we'd rather not call it."

Thomas acquired a pair of strong boots, whose toes he had to stuff with paper, and also a padded windbreaker, which, to Crutches' incredulity, fit him as if it had been made for him.

"You look normal. A proper wolf cub of the German Reich!"

Thomas fled when Crutches' jokes grew bitter. He didn't like Crutches then. Crutches' bitterness hurt him.

Nurse Monika was getting them ready for Christmas. She had decorated the tables in the barracks with pine branches and short, thick candles. She got little thanks for it from Crutches. He'd learned to avoid such celebrations. All a holiday meant to him was a lump in his throat and a miserable mood.

Nurse Monika was not to be diverted. It would be the first peacetime Christmas. He should just remember that.

"Oh, that too!" Crutches folded his hands and raised his eyes piously to the ceiling. "How deeply felt. Just don't ask me where I spent my last Christmas Eve. Or how."

She couldn't change his mood, and it became unnecessary.

The invisible organizations, the great dispersers, came to Crutches' rescue. No one had figured that any more transports would be organized before Christmas. Still, space had to be made, and on December 18 it was Thomas's and Crutches' turn. They knew their destination: Weisslingen.

It was a small city on the Neckar, they knew from Nurse Monika. They hadn't done badly. The place was supposed to have been spared by the war. Certainly Crutches would find work there without much difficulty. And Thomas could finally go to school again.

Then once again everything went much too quickly!

Then once again everyone talked at the same time.

Then there was packing and saying good-bye to everyone.

In the early morning the group walked across the courtyard. The snow squeaked under their shoes. The breath hung in front of their mouths in little clouds. Nurse Monika had insisted on accompanying them. It seemed to Thomas that he was walking in an old dream. Again, like the first long journey, it all seemed a little unreal. He felt free as a bird and invulnerable.

This time the transport consisted of only five cars. Since they weren't called and could choose their own car, Thomas managed to capture a corner without any trouble.

There was plenty of space, which caused Crutches to praise the generous transport command. "They didn't want to make Santa Claus angry," he scoffed. "Around this season even the pencil pushers get feelings."

Nurse Monika gave Crutches a fat kiss before she pulled him into the car with Thomas's help. She does like him, Thomas thought.

When the train started, they sat rolled in their blankets. The air blasted them to blocks of ice.

"I'm curious as to how they're going to melt us at the end of the journey. With hot air or with a Bunsen burner."

Thomas knew Crutches well enough by now. He knew that for the rest of the day he wouldn't say another word and had closed himself off in a kind of hibernation. Perhaps, he thought, Crutches was afraid that someone would become fond of him. It was like the melting Crutches had mentioned. Thomas knew Crutches wouldn't want to be completely melted.

Thomas couldn't sleep. He was much too excited. Somewhere the train would stop forever, they would climb out of the boxcar and stay. In a room, in an apartment, in a house. There would be no more camps, no more transport commands.

But the train took its time. It dawdled and was frequently held up by stop signals.

It began to snow again. The fine flakes dusted through the cracks in the planking. Since everyone was trying to escape them, there was constant movement in the boxcar. Only Crutches leaned in his corner, motionless.

Like an Indian, Thomas decided, or an old trapper. Probably nothing got past him. But everyone thought he was dreaming.

All the same, against all expectations, they landed just about evening on a siding at the edge of the railroad station in Weisslingen. It was a small station, well kept, clean, and undamaged.

The people in the boxcar gathered their things together. Some crowded out of the inhospitable, snow-encrusted quarters with hopes of a warm place to stay.

They were bitterly disappointed.

The officials who ran helplessly back and forth on the platform reassured them. This one night they must remain in the boxcar, as regrettable as that was. Tomorrow they would be taken to a school. There they would learn more about everything, and then they would also be assigned to rooms and houses.

Many people burrowed dispiritedly into coats and blankets; others scolded and refused to climb into the boxcar again.

Crutches hadn't moved. Now the excitement seemed to invigorate him.

"Come on!" He pushed Thomas, got up, cursed over his stiffened limbs, pulled up his coat collar, and yanked his cap down over his forehead.

"What's the point of quibbling over one night? We're there. At last. So let's go out and look around Weisslingen."

No one stopped them. They walked through dark, deserted streets. There were few streetlights to illuminate anything. Not one single house had been destroyed. The war had left no traces behind in this place. All at once Thomas felt foreign and dirty and shut out. Was Crutches feeling the same way?

They crossed a square with an iron fountain in the middle. There was no water coming out of it. Probably it was turned off because of the cold. The whole place seemed shut down, frozen. There was no one about. The houses hemmed the street with their closed shop shutters, dark and unwelcoming.

When they finally spied a light at the end of a narrow street, they began to run. It pulled them forward, promised warmth, life.

Breathless, they arrived at a square that astonished Thomas. It wasn't large. It was ringed with old, solid buildings. The light of two lanterns was lost in the spreading branches of a gigantic tree. Another light reached him, many-colored and looking incredibly festive as it streamed from the windows of a church in which the choir had taken their places.

It seemed to Thomas that the towering building was floating, a ship that not only shimmered but poured out music and voices.

Crutches leaned against the tree and took off his cap, as if he had already entered the church. The unexpected sight started him talking. "Boy, boy, what star have they sent us to? What time have we wandered into? Wasn't there shooting going on just a while back? Weren't we just sitting in a cattle car and thinking that we were human even so? Is that possible? Here we've been shuffling through a city whose inhabitants probably fear us like the plague. They've barricaded their houses and don't want to see us, don't want to know about us. They're practicing for Christmas Eve, our future hosts."

"Should we go in?" asked Thomas.

"No," Crutches decided. "We'll disturb their peace of mind. Better by day, when you can look them in the eye. When the store windows aren't closed any longer."

Without hurrying, they made their way back. Crutches gave an account to the people in the boxcar in his own way. They'd just come from another star, he said. Had anyone seen him and Tom? They were unable to make any contact with the inhabitants. They were either hibernating or protecting themselves from the foreign intruders. Finally he said, rubbing his hands, "They haven't lighted any celebration bonfires for us. So we'll have to prepare ourselves for it to be quite cold for a while yet."

The next day they were transferred to the school.

Friendly Schwabian-speaking officials whom they could scarcely understand wrote down their names and furnished them with stew and peppermint tea.

The next day they were transferred to another school.

Pleased, Crutches observed that it was better heated. "We're making progress," he said.

On December 22 Crutches came out of the office to which they'd been conducted with a piece of paper and read out solemnly, "Zeishäuserstrasse Twelve, Wagner, gravel works. This, my dear boy, is our new address. At which we may be reached in future by relatives, friends, officials, true believers, and especially Bronka. We are, they assure me, expected—so let's go and check in."

They didn't have to take all their baggage. What they couldn't carry would be delivered in the next few days by vehicle. That was, as Thomas had found out, a light carriage pulled by two cows.

Crutches didn't find this rig remarkable. "Cows, my dear fellow, are not useful in the war effort, you see. On the other hand, horses were requisitioned by the army. Most of them were knocked off or have been eaten long since."

The house stood at the edge of a small lake. "That's where the gravel is dredged," said Crutches.

The lake was frozen. A few children were skating.

Thomas wondered who was using his skates now. With this thought he realized for the first time that the house in Brünn was certainly not standing empty.

Strangers had doubtless moved in. Perhaps a boy his age had settled into his room and had found the skates in the cupboard in the front room.

When they got to the front door, Crutches took a deep breath. "Let's be surprised. We can celebrate or complain later!"

He rang. Nothing happened. After a decent interval, Crutches rang a second time. Now they heard doors slamming in the house, and voices. The door opened a crack. They saw a round, pleasant, woman's face. The round mouth opened only a little for a sound to which they knew no answer.

"Nahepya?"

"We—" Crutches started in. He got no further. The woman narrowed the space between door and frame to a slit through which she peeked and once again gave out this sound, a trace more understandably. "C'nah hepya?"

"We've been assigned to you. My name is Eberhard Wimmer. This is Thomas."

"Sright."

The woman opened the door with obvious reluctance.

"Wagner," she murmured. Still she didn't go so far as to bring them into her house but asked them to take a seat on the bench in the hall.

"Yull bin th'attic." And she assured them they needn't wait long.

They waited forever. Herr Wagner came, inspected them from a proper distance, murmured a greeting. Children ran past, staring at Crutches and Thomas as if they had giraffe necks and purple hair. Thomas, who couldn't tell one from another, was finally convinced that there must be at least a dozen Wagner children.

Eventually they reassured their involuntary hosts. There was talk behind closed doors.

Crutches stretched out his leg. "I wouldn't call this reception exactly friendly! Maybe they don't want to have us at all, my boy. Christmas is upon us. If they chuck us out, I'll play Joseph and you Mary."

"And the baby Jesus?"

"He's always there."

"How do you mean that, Crutches?"

Since Herr Wagner came in just then, Crutches never got around to explaining it to him. Herr Wagner wanted to see Crutches' identification.

"You don't trust us?" Crutches handed him his papers.

Herr Wagner responded with a sound like the one his wife had uttered earlier, "Y' cnna know," and disappeared, together with the papers.

The time stretched out. Still they continued to be

discussed, judging by the various sounds in the next room.

Crutches maintained his calm with difficulty. His leg began to jerk back and forth.

For sure, his phantom is paining him now, thought Thomas.

Frau Wagner released them. She said, "All right," and she was immediately understandable for the first time. After she'd given Crutches his papers back, she accompanied both the "assignees" to the attic.

Crutches had to bend when he entered the door into a room that was as wide as it was long. Three steps in any direction. The few pieces of furniture were crowded together. It was a riddle to Thomas how they were supposed to live here, unless one of them withdrew into the lopsided wardrobe.

Crutches appeared to be of another opinion. Obviously despair made him more cheerful.

"One bed, a wardrobe, one table, one chair," he stated. "As if that were nothing! Only"—smiling, he turned to Frau Wagner—"all that's missing is a second bed and—I don't want to make excessive demands—perhaps also a second chair."

Frau Wagner, who had pulled back into the corridor, knew what to say. "There's a second mattress on the bed, together with linen, and that can be laid on the floor at night. A second chair isn't necessary, since one of you can sit on the bed. For the rest, there should be a fire in the stove."

"How generous!" Crutches bowed and, hanging on the crutches, managed a gentle swing and closed the door just as gently. Then he let himself drop onto the bed, lighted a cigarette, looked searchingly around him, and nodded, obviously satisfied. "I'd really have been surprised if there were an ashtray here."

They settled in as well as they could.

The next day Crutches became very busy with something. He ordered Thomas to arrange the wardrobe and to create as much free space in their den as possible.

Crutches came and went. He'd obviously taken Frau Wagner into his confidence. Thomas heard them talking together in whispers in the hall. Frequently Crutches interrupted her with a friendly and insistent, "What did you just say?"

Gradually Thomas began to understand. Crutches was getting ready for Christmas. He was doing it in his own way. He organized. Even in Weisslingen he must already have stumbled on "sources." Whenever he returned, blue in the face with cold, his linen bag was stuffed full. He stowed his treasures in a box and forbade Thomas to look inside it. "No one looks in a hamster's cheeks," he said.

Thomas didn't have to be told. He wanted to be

surprised. He hoped that Crutches would stay happy and busy and divert him from a melancholy that gripped him ever more strongly and that he couldn't fight off. Mother hadn't been out of his thoughts the whole time. He'd been counting on seeing her again soon. Now he longed for her. This longing spread so painfully throughout his chest that he had trouble getting his breath. He meant to keep Crutches from noticing. But Crutches wasn't deceived and had known for a long time.

When they lay next to each other in the dark, Crutches propped up in bed and Thomas down on the floor on the mattress, Crutches began to speak.

"Are you asleep already, Tom? A stupid question. I know you're lying awake and staring at the ceiling that you can't even see. That's one thing about holidays. You can age a few years on an evening they still call holy. Suddenly you feel you're the only one in all humanity who's alone, because you're longing for someone you love who isn't there. That's the way it is now, right?"

Crutches' hand probed along the edge of the mattress, caught Thomas's earlobe, and then began to rub his back.

"It's not bad for you to be sad. But I would like to spare you aging before your time. If it only concerned me, Christmas Eve tomorrow would be just like any other day. Equally bleak, equally merry. But it concerns you, and now you go to sleep. And if you have to cry into the pillow, then cry for me, too. In spite of that, you can still have a little fun tomorrow."

Crutches had decided to change Christmas Eve into Christmas Eve Day. "A genuine little holiday," he proclaimed when they got up. "Genuine surprises and genuine happiness!"

It began with breakfast. Crutches got busy at the stove and set on it a pan in which something was bubbling and smelling wonderful. "Just get a whiff of this, Tom! Sit down, close your eyes. Expect paradise!"

His hamster trips had paid off. From dried milk and a piece of chocolate he had conjured up a drink for which, as he solemnly declared, there was yet no name. "Don't try to call this drink cocoa. You'd be a philistine and I would have nothing more to do with you." He talked like an opera singer gone berserk.

They quaffed and praised the refreshment, and Crutches announced the next festivity. "Now we wrap ourselves in our furs. Naturally we first clear the table, as is the custom with civilized travelers. Now, into the furs! And get set for a long walk. For in fact we are going to visit the municipal forest and steal a Christmas tree."

Crutches stood in front of Thomas in his flapping coat, the cap tilted and jaunty on his head. "Should we be apprehended by foresters, police, or any other officials, there will be another, entirely unplanned program feature ahead of us—jail."

"Oh, Crutches!" Thomas butted his head against Crutches' chest affectionately.

As they went along, Crutches described the district in such a way that Thomas wasn't sure whether he'd really learned so much about the place in the short time they'd been there or whether he was plainly and simply inventing. "The natives call the hill that we are now climbing so effortlessly Gallows Hill. Here not long ago were hanged thieves, murderers, witches, strangers, and people like us, i.e., Christmas tree swipers—hanged unhesitatingly and without mercy. Heavyweights escaped with their lives, since the frugal Weisslingers used only rotten rope. See there," Crutches pointed to a hollow in the snow with his crutch. "There they jumped from the gallows and left those dents, which in the vernacular are called gallows bumps."

"I don't believe that, Crutches."

"Let it go."

At the summit the wind drove tiny ice needles into their faces. Fairly exhausted, they reached the woods and began to look for a small tree. Crutches insisted they spare some half-grown straight little tree and seek out a small cripple that had nothing to celebrate in its tree life. Shortly thereafter they stumbled on just such a one, not quite knee-high, stunted and bent. "Just what we wanted," Crutches said.

The wind at their backs drove them straight home, where Crutches placed the tree in a flowerpot that had been filled with earth beforehand.

"We'll decorate it later," he said, and he began to bustle so busily around the little room that Thomas fled to the bed and watched his activity from there.

Crutches shaved. He got water from the bathroom, filled a kettle, placed it on the stove, blew on the fire, breathing hard, dug some potatoes out of the carton, peeled them with a flourish, cut them small, reported that quite by chance he'd discovered a sausage along with the potatoes, bit off the end, chewed, rolled his eyes, cut the sausage into slices, threw the potatoes into the water, threw the little wheels of sausage in after them, sniffed the steam, kept looking triumphantly at Thomas, salted, peppered, had even gotten hold of a little packet of paprika somewhere for seasoning, and—at the end of the cooking perform-

ance—invited Thomas to a one-of-a-kind potato gou-
lash, altogether unique in its own time and legendary
in later ages.

"It tastes fabulous."

"Oh, Crutches."

After the meal Crutches ordained bed and holiday
rest, which he proposed to sweeten with an advance
present. "Only don't think, pal"—he fished a book
out of the inexhaustible box and handed it to
Thomas—"that you're getting this present with no
strings attached. So as not to disturb my sleep, you
will kindly lie quietly on your mattress. To make it
easier for you, you can read."

Thomas did. He lay on his stomach and opened the
book. It was Erich Kästner's *Emil and the Detec-
tives.* He read the first page, and the second, forgot
Crutches, even forgot the holiday, and followed the
fleeing pickpocket with his friend Emil Tischbein.

Crutches snatched him back to reality. "Save
something for this evening, Tom. Our tree is waiting
to be decorated."

At home he was never allowed to be there during
the decorating and only saw the tree for the first time
when the lights were lit.

Crutches rooted from the box a few colored paper
stars, a gilded nut, and two candles. "We have to

parcel all this out so cleverly that it looks properly abundant."

Which, Thomas thought, they managed to do. With arms dangling, they stood in front of the little tree. Crutches tried to put on a pious expression but looked desperate instead.

"And now?" asked Thomas, to help him out of his embarrassment.

"And now we go downstairs and wish the many-headed gravel-pit-owning family of Wagners Merry Christmas and are curious to see what they make of it."

Frau Wagner invited them into the kitchen, talked much—probably in embarrassment—fast and incomprehensibly, and invitingly held out to Thomas a plate heaped with cookies.

"Merry Christmas," she said, "even if the circoomstanshes an't very nice. And may the guudies taste guude."

They thanked her.

They didn't see a single one of the other Wagners.

"Do you know what these are?" asked Thomas, placing the plate under the tree.

Crutches made his mouth round and blew. "Guudies."

They tasted marvelous, and Crutches added

thoughtfully, "Maybe Frau Wagner is a decent human being at heart. It's just that we've been billeted on her, as sort of a rear guard of Hitler's war, strangers and apparently without resources. How could we expect that the two of us would be welcome?"

As if he'd spoken the last line in a theatrical scene, Crutches snapped off the light. They stood in the dark. "Light the candles, Tom," he said softly. "The matches are on the windowsill."

In the light of the two candles the crippled little tree grew and became beautiful. They looked and were silent. Crutches laid his arm across Thomas's shoulders and wavered a little on his leg. After a while he said, "We're still a little bit more comfortable than in the stall in Bethlehem."

He let go of Thomas.

"Now one surprise will follow the next. Sit down and close your eyes!"

Thomas heard him hopping here and there. Paper rustled. Metal banged against metal.

"You can look now!"

Right in front of him, on the table under the tree, lay ice skates. They glittered in the candlelight, looking utterly unreal. Carefully he reached toward them.

Crutches drew excitedly on his cigarette. "Well?"

"Thank you," said Thomas. He closed his eyes again. Behind the closed lids the skates continued to glimmer.

Music sounded far away.

Now I'm going crazy, Thomas thought.

The music came nearer, became louder; Crutches' voice mixed with it. "The second gigantic surprise! A present from Crutches for Tom and Crutches."

Thomas stared unbelievingly at the little box—a radio! "How did you manage that, Crutches?"

From the radio, bells began to sound.

"My dear fellow, I never expected such a vulgar question from you."

"But . . ."

"Take it easy. The radio isn't stolen and didn't involve any shady deals. I got credit."

"I don't believe you, Crutches."

Crutches sat on the bed. In his eyes were tiny reflections of the two candles. "Whether you do or not, on this evening, which is supposed to be a holy one, you have to believe it."

They listened to the radio. They ate Frau Wagner's guudies with enjoyment. And after they had arranged the mattress for the night, Thomas read some more.

It was late when Crutches turned out the light.

"Crutches," said Thomas, "today was wonderful."

"I thought so too."

But Thomas didn't tell him that all the surprises and pleasure had not lessened the pain in his heart.

"Good night, Crutches."

"Good night, Tom. Tomorrow you can try out your skates."

◆

F I F T E E N
Farewell

In the course of the next eight months they changed quarters four times. Crutches named the places after the seasons: The Winter Digs at Wagners'; Spring Sojourn at the farmer's in Neckarstotzingen, where Thomas learned the basic vowels of the Schwabian dialect and Crutches tried to learn to drink milk; the Summer Room in the attic in Marktstrasse, in which Crutches dried large tobacco leaves on the clothesline; and finally the real apartment, the Autumn Palace in Jusistrasse. It consisted of two rooms, a cooking niche, and a real bathroom, which they celebrated as the greatest luxury of all. And into which in the first few weeks Crutches retreated for interminably long periods of sitting.

Thomas had now been going to school for six

months. He found a friend, Gerd, to study with and to hang around with. Crutches encouraged him to study. Certainly he'd learned a great deal of life in his year out of school, but he still had to catch up as quickly as he could in math, English, and Latin.

In the beginning Thomas found it difficult to stay alone in his room for very long. He preferred to sit around with Crutches or go outside and wander around through the city alone or with Gerd. He still felt the restlessness of the long journey.

Crutches had found work. He supposed that during his frequent visits to the housing office he'd appeared so regularly that they'd just kept him there. As often as he had gone on angrily about bureaucrat jackasses, he was now one of them himself.

It was a great relief for them both, because somehow Crutches had managed to get assigned to the child welfare office. So now Thomas was "officially" allowed to stay with Crutches.

He heard nothing from Mother. She was missing. Crutches checked regularly with the Red Cross and each time came home without any news.

"She'll turn up soon, Tom. She had to get to somewhere too. Like us. Then she'll look for you."

Sometimes Tom dreamed of Mother, but her face was always obscure, even when she came closer, as if it were blotted out. He said nothing to Crutches about it. Otherwise somehow Crutches might get the idea that Thomas liked Mother more than him. Perhaps that was so. And perhaps not. For Thomas needed Crutches and was very fond of him.

Even though he quarreled with him now and again, especially about whose week it was to wash the stairs or who should dry the dishes. Even when he lay awake deep into the night sometimes, waiting for Crutches, who came home tipsy and made fun of his anxiety. And even when Crutches accused him of being lazy and messy and yet still avoided doing his own household tasks.

These were trivialities. They got on well with each other, trusted each other. They had a home, the Autumn Palace. They had finally arrived.

And yet not.

When, after nearly a year had passed since their arrival in Weisslingen, a damp snow announced the beginning of winter, something happened with Crutches.

At first Thomas assumed that the foul weather had made him out of sorts and perhaps he'd begun to feel the phantom pain in his leg. But Crutches was acting much too crazy and too enigmatic for that. He was feeling lousy, he admitted, that was true, but there was nothing wrong with him.

He pulled one surprise after another on Thomas.

One time he would torture him with hour-long si-
lences, then again he'd take him to the movies and
talk all the way home without stopping. One time he
hugged Thomas for no reason, then again he threw a
cooking spoon at him and scolded him for being a
slovenly rattle-brain who couldn't take any responsi-
bility.

One evening Thomas couldn't bear it any longer.
He felt like yelling and punching Crutches.

Crutches had come home from work, punctually as
always. But he didn't say anything and didn't ask, as
he usually did, what Thomas had done and seen.
Nothing, not one word. He let his leg drag across the
floor as if his crutches had gotten shorter. Wordlessly
he warmed up the evening meal. Wordlessly he sat at
the table. Wordlessly he cleaned up. Thomas looked
at him and didn't dare speak to him. He was afraid
Crutches would fly into a gigantic rage, for he looked
dangerous and sad at the same time. Pale, dark rings
under his eyes, hair straggling over his forehead.
Probably he's gotten into a mess at the office,
Thomas thought. Made some kind of terrible mistake.

Crutches pulled the chair over to the little chest on
which the radio stood, turned it on. They were broad-
casting serious music. Crutches closed his eyes.

Thomas was certain he wasn't listening to it. That
he was thinking about something. On tiptoe he
slipped into his room. He lay down on his bed and
tried to read; though he racked his brains, he found
no explanation for Crutches' condition. He'd never
yet seen him this way. So rejecting, so hurt and taci-
turn.

In the next room, Crutches kept playing the grave,
solemn music, his mourning music.

Thomas slipped under the blanket. There was no
stove in his room. When the door was closed, it got
cold quickly. Phrases came to him from Bronka's
letter that had come a few days before. In it she said
good-bye. She was traveling with the next group of
children to the Promised Land, to Jerusalem. She
planned to remain there. She'd written a couple of
particularly loving lines especially to Crutches.
Thomas knew them almost by heart. "That you'll
protect Tom like the apple of your eye I know very
well. But you must still take care of yourself, too, my
dearest one-leg among all the two-legs. You think
your strength is inexhaustible and that your lion's
heart will never grow weak. I won't take this belief
from you, but I do just ask you to husband your
strength. If you won't do it for yourself, then do it for
us. We need you."

Thomas spoke the last sentence aloud. Why hadn't Crutches taken Bronka's letter to heart the way he had? If Crutches had, he wouldn't be behaving this way. He repeated Bronka's lines, spoke them to oppose the music in the next room and the Crutches who'd become a stranger. He fell asleep with the words on his lips.

A hand waked him. It lay on his, moved gently back and forth. He wasn't dreaming. It had to be Crutches. Crutches had come to him after this dreadful evening.

"Crutches?"

"Yes."

"Are you feeling better?"

"Yes."

"Then what's the matter? Did you have a fight with your boss?"

Crutches laughed to himself, the bed shook. "Certainly not. He understands me."

"Are you sick?"

"Yes, something like that. Hurt, way inside. Slide over to the wall a little bit, and give me a piece of your blanket, will you? An icehouse has nothing on your room."

Crutches slipped in next to him. He didn't let go of Thomas's hand.

Only during the long train ride, when they'd been afraid they were going to freeze to death, had they bundled together under the two blankets to share each other's warmth. Never since. Thomas would have thought it weird. But tonight they again needed each other's warmth, as they had then.

"We need you," Thomas whispered. He lay on his back and felt for Crutches' arm.

"Bronka exaggerated," Crutches muttered.

"No, it's true. You're no judge at all."

"Aren't I?" Crutches took a deep breath.

"No."

Thomas hesitated, searching for the right words. He didn't want to anger Crutches or hurt him.

"Why did you say that you're hurt?"

"I intended not to tell you until tomorrow. I can't hold out." He pressed Thomas's hand so hard that it hurt. "I've been keeping something from you, Tom, and I feel myself in your debt. I feel like a swine. Don't say anything. Just listen, if you can. I've known for two weeks. For two weeks I've been carrying it around with me, breakfasting with you, eating with you at noon, spending most evenings with you, and I should have told you long ago. But I, dizzy sentimental fool, wanted to have these two weeks left for me."

Thomas caught his breath. That was why Crutches didn't seem to know what to do. He'd had a fight with the child welfare office. Probably they wouldn't let Crutches keep him anymore. He sat up. "Is it something with the office? Do I have to leave?"

Crutches pulled him back onto the pillow. "No, I haven't had any trouble with the office; they're satisfied with us. But you do have to leave. To go to your mother."

"To Mother?"

Crutches' hand closed firmly and yet very gently on his arm. Thomas lay still. Thoughts and beginnings of sentences tumbled together in his head. That's not true, he thought. Crutches said, "To Mother." Perhaps he didn't say it at all, perhaps I'm just imagining it.

"I've known for two weeks." Crutches spoke softly, hesitantly, as if he were reading aloud a story that he didn't yet know. "She was looking for you, too. The Red Cross in Munich found you through our search bulletins. Your mother is living there now. I've spoken with her on the telephone. We've arranged that we'll meet tomorrow—no," Crutches corrected himself, "it's already today—in the railroad station in Stuttgart, and she'll take you back."

A voice in his head cried, "Mama!" It was the boy

in Kolin, who'd wandered through the mass of people, beside himself with desperation. He was happy and at the same time felt terrible anxiety. "Will you go too?"

"Of course. I'm taking you to Stuttgart."

Thomas turned to Crutches and laid his arm across his chest. "I mean, to Munich?"

"No, Tom. I have work here. Your mother will certainly want to have you to herself after this long time."

Now grief and fear pushed aside his joy. He pressed against Crutches. "Then won't we ever see each other again?"

"Nonsense. I'll come visit you. You and your mother. And we'll write letters. So, old fellow, I'll manage to think about myself sometimes. That's something."

Nothing helped. Not that he heard Crutches speaking, that he crept close to him, that he asked him about his phantom leg. He didn't want to cry, but it broke out of him. It hurt and it felt good. And it tired him out. Even in half sleep he noticed that Crutches kept rubbing his arm over his face. He's crying too, Thomas thought.

Crutches let him sleep and only wakened him when it was time. The suitcase stood all packed.

"You mustn't forget your blanket, Bronka's parting gift. Do you want to roll it yourself, the way you did on the transport?" Thomas could still do it just as fast as he could then; he hadn't lost the knack.

His whole body was tense. Every step hurt as he walked along beside Crutches.

The train left promptly. They had only forty-five minutes left. They sat beside each other in the compartment. He kept looking at Crutches from the side. Crutches was silent, chewing on his cigarette. Thomas wanted to talk with Crutches, to tell him how marvelous he thought he was, how he loved him. Crutches' unyielding silence and the attentiveness of the people who sat in the compartment with them kept him from doing it. He didn't even dare grasp Crutches' hand.

Before the train stopped, they were already standing at the door.

Crutches got out first.

Thomas followed him, took the suitcase, the blanket.

He heard a short scream, then he saw her. She hadn't changed at all. She had simply come back again after she'd been away for a while. Now he ran too. He ran right at her. She caught him; she smelled familiar and spoke with a voice that he had missed, of which he'd dreamed. She rocked him. "You've gotten big," she said. "You look well," she said. "My God," she said.

It was a long time before she let him go.

He looked around for Crutches. He'd disappeared. "Crutches!" he cried.

Mother held him fast. "He wanted it this way, Thomas. We arranged it this way. He didn't want to make the parting harder for you, your Crutches."

She'd said, "Your Crutches."

"We've arranged that he'll come and visit us soon."

"Really?"

"Yes." She ran her hand over his head, carefully, as if she had to learn it again.

"We still have a lot of time before our train leaves. Perhaps we can find a place in the waiting room where we can sit. And to make the time pass, you have to tell me. Everything."

"Yes," he said. And he thought, Suddenly I just saw him, suddenly there he was, hopping along on his crutches in front of me. It was very warm there.

PETER HÄRTLING

is a lecturer, journalist, editor, and publisher whose experiences during World War II compelled him to write *Crutches*. He was born in Chemnitz, which is now behind the Iron Curtain and called Karl-Marx-Stadt. He writes that in 1945, when he was twelve years old, his childhood came to an end. His father, a lawyer and anti-Nazi who was drafted into the German army, died in a Russian prison. He and his mother and sister fled to Austria to avoid living in Russian-occupied territory. A year later, despondent at the loss of her husband and the cruelty of daily life, his mother committed suicide, leaving him and his sister to survive the aftermath of war alone.

Peter Härtling now lives with his wife and four children in Mörfelden-Walldorf, Federal Republic of Germany.

ELIZABETH D. CRAWFORD

is highly regarded for her translations from German which include *Hansel and Gretel, Little Red Cap,* and *The Seven Swans* by Lisbeth Zwerger, and *Don't Say a Word* by Barbara Gherts. Ms. Crawford lives in Connecticut.